THREE

GRAY

DOTS

K.L. RANDIS

THREE
GRAY
DOTS

To my daughters.

You have one heart and many choices to make.

Let your heart guide you, but your choices define you.

You are both my greatest loves.

Prologue

The second time I witnessed Jackson attempt to kill himself, he was standing at the ocean's edge with a .22 in his right hand.

The September breeze whipping off the clashing waters, mixed with the darkened skies as the sun began to set, told me that we would be alone for a while. I squinted down the coastline anyway, hoping someone would be flying a kite or walking a dog and would witness what was about to happen.

There was no one.

A softer, seaweed-colored haze surrounded his blank pupils. They were a lot like his personality, a mixture of steel and cotton that didn't know how to coexist together.

At that moment the structural frame that kept him together was unfolding.

Jackson's shoulders were hunched as if he was about to get sick—adrenaline stemming from my showing up to the beach moments before he off'ed himself seemed to shake his confidence in what he had been planning to do.

"You told me this would get easier," he whispered, his eyes locked with mine. He turned his head toward the water, a flicker of air pushing dark strands of hair across his forehead. For a moment I considered grabbing the gun and heaving it as far as I could into the depths of the ocean. I knew better. He would find another way, any way, to end the pounding in his head. He was barely thirty but had a chiseled physique and a fast mile. He'd be head first into the ocean within seconds to find the gun at that point. If he didn't find it, he would simply choose not come up for air.

Right then, I was his air.

"I did say that," I confessed. "This isn't you." I nodded toward the gun. "I know you."

"You don't know anything!"

I flinched as angst forced his trembling hands to rest on the top of his head, the .22 pointed inadvertently in my direction.

In response, I lowered myself to the chilled sand. Patting a spot beside me, I lured him to do the same. His body language told me he would never let me in that easy, but if I could get sand into his hands, I could distract him enough from the agony his face was telling me he felt.

"Do you know what today is?" he asked, wiping his nose on his sleeve and coughing to cover up the pitch in his voice.

"I do."

"I don't know who I am anymore," he muttered, more to himself. The wind threatened to drown out anything else he said, so I patted the spot next to me with one hand while letting sand drift through my fingers like an hourglass in the other. He watched the crystallized strands flow to the ground, sighing deeply.

That's it, come back to me now.

One knee bent behind him and the next one followed, bringing the gun to rest on his right thigh. Shoulders still hunched, he refused to look at me.

I mistakenly reached out to touch his left thigh and he flinched, looking up and then back down at my hand.

I turned my palm toward him. "Feel the sand with me," I suggested. I was unsure if he could hear the thudding in my chest over the wind.

2

He stared at me for a moment, then back down at my open hand. Nodding, he rubbed his beard before inching his fingers toward mine.

When our hands interlocked, I put pressure around his fingers and started to bury our hands beneath the cold surface of the sand like a squirrel. Once our hands were mostly covered, we took turns squeezing the sand between each other's fingers in a slow and rhythmic motion.

"You know why I'm doing this?" I asked, knowing that he wouldn't look at me when he answered.

"To bring me back," he replied.

"Yes." I shook my head and we sat in silence a few minutes longer, watching the waves stealthily inch closer.

"Hey, why are *you* crying?" Jackson's voice alerted me to the trickle of tears that were being supplied by the adrenaline.

"I'm okay."

"You're not."

"I don't know either," I confessed.

"Huh?"

"You said earlier that you don't know who you are anymore."

He nodded.

"I don't either," I whispered.

With our hands interlocked beneath the sand, he had no choice but to let the gun slide down his thigh and fall in-between us so that he could cup my chin in his hand. "We've been here before, haven't we?" he asked.

The burn from trying to hold back tears was evident on my face, I was sure. "Yes, Jackson. We've been here before."

"So what happened? Why are we here again? What did we do wrong this time so that we're right back to where we started?"

"It's not anyone's fault. We didn't do anything wrong, we just..."

"We just what?" he asked, his breath lingering on my lips.

I closed my eyes, trying to fight the urge to do what I knew I shouldn't do. "We can't do this."

"We can," he coaxed.

His leaned on his free hand so that our noses were almost touching. The sun had disappeared long ago and the only way we could make out the shapes of each other was courtesy of the stars peeking out from above. "We can do this, we can fix it."

"I don't know if we can..." Shifting my weight, I used my shoulder to gently push against his chest so I could breathe, so I could give myself the space I needed to think clearly.

"Pippa, I love you."

My knee-jerk response to him telling me he loved me for the first time flew out of my mouth. "There's no way you can."

"You have no idea, Pip. I've loved you from the moment I saw you, you have to know that."

"You can't love me," I demanded.

"Why not?" he asked, the desperation in his voice mimicking my own.

"Because you have no idea who I really am," I said. I closed my eyes, not knowing if what I was about to say was going to help or hurt the situation. "I've been lying to you this whole time."

Chapter 1

"What is that distressing noise coming from room two-thirty-three?" I asked, craning my neck around the nurse's station and down the hallway of Palmetto Hospital's mental health unit.

"New guy," Lisa replied, not looking up from her phone as she scrolled through Facebook. "Well, not *new*. He's spent twenty-four hours in the emergency room already but they transferred him to our lovely section of housing accommodations. Apparently he had a rough night."

"He didn't have a rough night," Moe chimed in. "He gave Victoria a rough night. He punched her right in the face when she went in around two a.m. to take his vitals."

"Noooooo," I replied. "Is that why she's not here today? I didn't think she was the kind of intern to call it quits after day four but if she had a night like that..."

"He's a menace," Lisa said. "Stay away unless you absolutely need to go in there."

"Speaking of that," Moe said, "who's going in next? They removed his restraints early this morning but I don't know..."

Eyes still glued to her phone Lisa smiled. "I'll rock-paper-scissors you for it."

I rolled my eyes and made my way down the hall to start rounds as Moe pushed his chair across the floor to get closer to Lisa. As I flipped through my charts I could hear them slapping their fists together behind me, with Moe ultimately objecting. "Hey, best two out of three, Lisa. You cheated!"

"I got it guys, don't want you to work too hard," I called over my shoulder.

"Might want to put some scrubs on first," Moe teased.

"Might want to take a long walk off a short pier," I replied.

"He's not your patient!" Lisa called after me.

"I don't see you jumping up to check on him," I said, raising an eyebrow. "It'll take me two minutes. You can thank me by buying me lunch later."

I exhaled slowly, regretting the second cup of coffee I had finished in the elevator moments before my shift started. My mission to make it to work with enough time to eat a decent meal from the cafeteria almost never happened, so a cup or three of coffee usually fueled me enough until I could sneak away for a salad or muffin at lunch time.

Moe and Lisa usually managed to push through their mornings on energy drinks and clementines, so at least they would speak to their first patients smelling like orange juice instead of a stale coffee house.

I managed to not eat anything that morning, and I was also still in my street clothes since a forgotten pen in one of my pockets anointed the only clean scrubs I had managed to transfer into my dryer after a grueling fifteen hour shift the day before. Lisa was kind enough to give me her locker combo so I could steal a pair of her scrubs for my shift, but I was late as it was and needed to at least make an appearance to one patient on the floor before I changed. The life of a psychiatric nurse was an immersive one with exiguous pauses.

The halls of Palmetto's mental health unit were often barren, even though we were a mere twenty-nine minute drive to the Marine Corps base Camp Lejeune. We were one of three hospitals in the area that had a dedicated inpatient facility for psychiatric holds that were funneled through the emergency room. We specialized in treating veterans, given our proximity to the Marine base. Patients were categorized— unofficially, and by the nurses who worked the unit—into one of three designated groups: *Desperates*, *Fireworks*, or *Sads*.

We'd never admit it to our Charge Nurse, but before each shift we'd secretly update each other on the status of the newbies who had come in or on the ones being released. It made working the floor slightly more predictable, although the word 'predictable' was a unicorn word in our unit.

Desperates were comprised of impulsive individuals who would hit rock bottom without warning. They were pill-swallowers, self-mutilators, and suicide-note-writers. They'd usually show up accompanied by a loved one, only to be discharged several hours to two days later and with a newfound appreciation for life outside of hospital food and one-on-one deep breathing lessons. Most times they were the ones that would never return. The ones that did ultimately show up again would wait until tensions built up so powerfully that no breathing techniques would slow their minds.

Fireworks were a hit-or-miss bunch that either threw feces at us when we entered their rooms or blankly stared at the aging ceiling tiles for weeks. Carl was the first patient I had who fooled me into thinking I was any good at my job. When he was admitted he had been caught with his pants down at the grocery store, a full sized trout placed between his legs in the seafood aisle. Screaming to 'Free Willy' he ran, shrieking obscenities until the freshly waxed floor in aisle nine curtailed his fun by sending him slip-and-slide style into an end cap of Progresso soups.

Two days after he woke up, appearing lucid enough, he told me he had not remembered the grocery store incident and that he probably forgot to take his medication. After several sessions together, only twenty-four hours before I intended to hand in paperwork to my supervisor for his release, he managed to steal an extra pair of scrubs and make his way into another patient's room. Him and another *Firework* were happily cutting long incisions up their thighs, convincing each other that they were surgeons, and drawing pictographs of an imaginary patient's tumor on the walls with their own blood.

"Oh, Carl," I muttered under my breath, stopping in front of room two-thirty-three. Sunlight flooded the hall from the one lone window at the end as I turned the chart over in my hand. I dragged my finger down the center as I read, absorbing the vital information it handed over on who was behind the door: name, admission date and reason, some history. Raising an eyebrow I realized we were the same age, and I exhaled slowly, noticing the light scent of coffee still lingering. "Please don't punch me in the face," I said, pushing the door open.

My eyes couldn't adjust to the darkness, and it took me a moment to realize the patient had hung bed sheets on the windows to block out any additional light that came through. Unsure if anyone had seen me enter, I gently cleared my throat to announce my arrival.

"Anyone awake in here?" I asked, keeping my voice barely above a whisper.

Nothing.

I took three steps toward the bed, light from the hallway barely illuminating the brand new, white sneakers I purchased after a projectile vomit episode—courtesy of a *Desperate*—from a few days earlier. "I'm here to visit, is that okay?"

The bed sheets rustled and I remained where I was until I had permission to move any closer. Sometimes giving the patient some control, even a small amount, was all it took to break down a barrier and gain trust.

"Is she okay?" said a voice.

"Ohhh..." I said, covering my mouth before I finished reacting. I had never heard words spoken with such remorse in my life. They were laden with the kind of gruff undertone that suggested someone had been crying. The word 'okay' was barely dragged from the depths of his throat, pitching and breaking at just the right moment that made hairs on the back of my neck stand on edge.

A heap of sheets slowly rose from the bed into an upright position, shape-shifting into the outline of a man. "The nurse I punched in the face this morning, is she okay?"

I inched closer to the bed, searching my memory for the update on Victoria that Lisa had given me. "Yeah," I said. "I think she's okay."

He cleared his throat, as if to offer an explanation, but remained silent.

"How are you?" I asked.

I watched a hand rise from the sheets, coming to rest on his face. Cradling his forehead in his palm, knees bent and chest forward, the balled-up version of the man I thought was going to punch me initially was no longer a worry. I could tell he was looking in my direction from the weak swallows of light coming from the ajar door behind me.

"You know what I love about the dark?" he asked. The steadfast nature of his voice came out as a lullaby of words, strung together with so much pain that I hurt for him.

I swallowed in response, giving him the silence he needed to continue.

"It's forgiving," he said. "The dark consumes everything. If you can't see anything, it forces you to feel everything. It gives you a reason to stop and really feel the things you would otherwise shut out."

"What are you feeling right now?" I asked, pointing to the sheets hanging from the window. I wanted to match the softness of his voice when I spoke. It was alluring, and the contradiction of who I thought he was when I had first entered the room versus the shell of a man I saw in front of me made my head woozy.

"Everything," he replied finally. "I don't want to feel anything."

I closed my eyes at his response, thankful for the dim surroundings that hid my expression. "Seems to me you feel quite a bit," I responded. "At least that's how it looks from where I'm standing."

"Move closer."

"Sorry?"

"That's not true. If you come closer you'll see."

9

The same hairs from before stood up on the back of my neck and I tried to assess whether or not he was threatening me or trying to prove a point.

"I won't hurt you," he promised. "Just come closer so you can see for yourself."

Nodding, my sneakers shuffled over the floor toward the bed with reservation. When I was within an arm's distance from him, he patted the bed next to him.

"I don't think that's a good idea," I said.

"Please? Please sit."

Sighing, I glanced over my shoulder at the ajar door as I lowered myself onto the bed. Crossing my hands in my lap, I forced a smile. "I don't think—"

My hands covered my mouth to stifle my scream as his right hand sprung from the bed. Convinced I was about to be hit I kept my eyes closed, but the crack never came.

"Open your eyes," he demanded.

Adrenaline forced me to do as I was told, so I half-squinted before opening my eyes. Sunlight flooded the room, and I blushed when I realized his arm had outstretched to pull the sheets off of the window to let light in.

I met his eyes, and for a moment I was staring into a black hole. Hypnotizing hues of green and brown swirled around pupils that held no reason or emotion. Both arms were now placed slightly behind him, elbows locked, perching his body upright on the bed. A cascade of mountains presented themselves where his arms and chest were. He was a rock, in every sense of the word, robust and cold but breathtakingly solid. Lowering his beard to his chest and breaking eye contact with me, I followed his gaze down the crevices of his chest.

"I can tell you see it, the darkness" he said, keeping his chin tilted downward. "No one can ever see past it."

"No one can be dark all the time," I said, taking advantage of the fact that he was looking away from me. Studying his jawline I imagined him sunbathing on one of the beaches littered down the North Carolina shore where we were. Other than the hospital gown sagging over one arm of the chair next to us, there was no indication he belonged in a mental health unit.

"I'm here because I'm trying to feel *something*, because I *am* the dark."

"So let's keep the sheet down for a while to bring in the light. No one deserves to be in the dark all the time."

He sighed, bringing his elbows to rest on the tops of his knees. Staring at me he shook his head, and I couldn't ignore the skip in my chest.

The way he exposed his emotions was the most gorgeous thing I had ever seen in a man. I cringed at the cliché. I was guarded against the facade of alluring men, courtesy of past relationships that crippled any future chances of falling for the superficial.

He was mesmerizing.

Comfortable enough in his own skin, he preferred to sit in dark rooms and punch at walls that happened to be too close to nurse's faces. No one was at his bedside, and there were no flowers or cards in his room. He was truly alone in his fight, and the part of me that was telling my brain to stop wondering how soft his lips felt was the same part that inched my hand closer to his.

"Why not? What scares you about the light?" I asked.

He parted his lips, moving his face closer to mine and I could feel his breath cascade around me. "I can tell, just by looking at you, that you *are* the light. Someone like me would consume you." He nodded toward the door. "So go, and don't come back."

Moments later I pulled the door behind me, leaving room two-thirty-three almost in tears. Lisa looked up at me from down the hall and raised an eyebrow when she saw my face, advancing toward me as I stood immobilized in front of the closed door.

"What happened?" Lisa asked, eyeing the door. "Is he a *Firework* or a *Desperate*? Moe thinks he's a *Firework* but Helen on night shift said—"

"He's a *Sad*," I said, looking up at her.

"A what?"

"Jackson isn't a *Firework* or a *Desperate*, he's a *Sad*."

Lisa's eyes widened. "Jackson?"

"His name is Jackson," I said. "And I can't go back in there again."

Chapter 2

The Inlet served half-off clams and dollar beers on Sunday afternoons. I would show up thirty minutes after opening and claim my favorite spot, a table for two, in the far right corner that overlooked the ocean. It was a quiet, lesser-known spot on the main strip where locals frequented. The bartender knew most of the orders, people, and gossip about anyone who walked through the door.

It was an unusually warm day in January and only a sweatshirt was needed as temperatures hovered around the mid-fifties. I tilted my chin toward the water, salt drifting off of the ocean and fusing to my skin, as I wondered if anyone working at The Inlet would recognize me. Faded umbrellas in ocean-hued colors that were scattered among the tables fluttered in the wind, lazily rising and falling with the bursts of air that escaped the tide.

One unexpected gust wrestled with my hair in such a way that I scrambled to find a ponytail within the confines of my clutch. I had looped the barrette twice around my hair when Susan appeared, a mouth full of gum and a betraying smudge of chocolate lingering on the corner of her lip. "Oh!" she exclaimed when she saw me, "You're blonde now. What happened to the auburn?"

"Just wanted something different," I said, taking the beer she handed me. "Not good?"

She cocked her head to the side, studying me. "I think it's the best yet," she said, mostly to herself. "Yeah, I like it. I think you found your color. Clams? Or are we waiting for Meg?"

I glanced at my watch. "Give her ten more minutes. I told her noon so she should be here around twelve thirty."

She nodded, not bothering to write anything down. "We have some kind of new butter, you guys want to try it?"

"Depends. Did Ned make it?"

"Of course he did."

"Then of course we'll try it."

She headed toward the kitchen and I directed my attention to the ocean, only to hear a lowered voice speak out again.

"Pippa?"

I turned my head across the deserted deck, locking eyes with Susan. "I heard you made it to Fifth Avenue with your new goal time," she said. Her eyes glimmered at the idea that I could actually pull off qualifying for the Boston Marathon.

I nodded, sipping my water and smiling.

"Good for you, kid. I hope you get your letter soon," she said, winking and then disappearing into the restaurant.

Meg was always late. We would decide on a time and I would usually arrive half an hour before we said we'd meet. It guaranteed me a solid hour to sit by myself before she got there and I could just let the gravity of the ocean's presence consume me.

I hadn't known Meg my entire life, but she was the kind of girlfriend who dropped compliments left and right on anything that made you feel self-conscious about yourself. I was the kind of friend who gave Meg the kind of honest transparency no one ever bothered to show her. I never understood the power of having girlfriends who lifted you up, until Meg.

I remembered going to The Inlet for her birthday that first year we met. It was going well, until two Long Islands and various birthday shots from other locals put her face deep in a toilet sometime before midnight. I had grabbed her phone to call her on-again-off-again boyfriend to come pick her up and put her to bed, but accidentally drunk dialed *my* ex instead.

It was the greatest mistake of my life.

Waiting outside of the woman's bathroom, I watched him enter the bar twenty minutes later, his mouth twisting in a way that said he was angry but his eyes showing puddles of worry. I was drunk too, and I had long since forgotten what I had said on the phone that made him show up—he was not the chivalrous type—but there he was, my knight in shining armor.

"Is she in there?" he asked, eyeing me cautiously when he approached. I don't think he was entirely sure that I would be able to hold a conversation.

"Who?"

"Meg. Is your friend Meg still in there or not?"

His eyes were a teal blue, and distracting to the point that I forgot the question he had asked. Instead I wondered if the smear of eyeliner I knew I had resting under both eyes from crying earlier in the night about who-knows-what was still visible.

"I'm Pippa, not Meg," I said. I then immediately threw up all over his boots.

"You're thinking about Dylan again, you moron," Meg said, disrupting my trance as she sat down across from me.

"You're half an hour late, as always."

She placed her clutch on the table and cocked her head to one side, staring at me and half-blocking my view of the ocean. "You have a stupid smile and you're doing that Oscar the Grouch thing." She crinkled her nose and I watched her eyebrows cram together in an angry V in the middle of her face.

"You look ridiculous," I said, looking away as my face flared from embarrassment.

"Exactly. So stop doing it, Oscar. You order me a beer?"

15

"No Long Islands for you today?" I teased.

"See, I knew you were thinking about him. Knock it off, or I'll tattle on you to your mother."

"Don't go there," I warned.

"Oh, stop, you would have laughed at that if you were in a better mood" she exclaimed, throwing her hands up in the air. Susan appeared, placing a beer in front of Meg and walking away before she heard much else.

"Tell me one more time about the last time you saw him," I insisted.

"Pippa I don't *want to*. He shows up to the bar once in a blue moon and it's weird to feed you gossip about him," Meg whined. She stared at my blank face for a moment before sighing. "Sometimes Susan needs an extra hand behind the bar. He will show up every once in a while and order a beer or two and stare out at the ocean. He pays in cash, never talks to anyone, and he still has the craziest blue eyes I've ever seen in my life, much like mine." She batted them to drive home her point.

"So he's obviously fine, right? I mean he hasn't developed a personality disorder or run crying from the bar after a few drinks?"

"Well, not exactly." Her face drooped and she chugged half of her beer in response.

"Meg?" I said in my best mom-voice. "What are you leaving out?"

"I saw the look on his face when someone ordered a Long Island," she confessed, nodding. "I might have told him maybe he should call you."

"Meg!

"I know, but realistically the guy looks so shut down. Listen, you do that Pippa-thing where you ask without really asking so I tell you, without really telling you. You want updates on Dylan because you want to know how he's doing, I get it, but if you want to know so bad why don't you just ask him yourself? It's the same song and dance every time after almost a year of you guys splitting up and it's exhausting. So if you're not interested in doing your own detective work that's fine, I just wanted to skip that part right now because I think we have better things to talk about, don't you?"

Narrowing my eyes at her I nodded, watching a slow smile spread across her face. "Dude, hello!" she exclaimed. "You got to Fifth Avenue within your goal time and didn't think to call your best friend? Why'd I have to hear it from Susan?"

"It's not a big deal," I responded.

"Of course it's a big deal, you've spent the past year chugging along Main Street and now you're finally breaking your best running times. You're going to be a roadrunner in that marathon before you know it. Did you tell your mom?"

"What?" I asked, rubbing my right earlobe.

"I said did you tell your mom?"

"Huh?" I responded. I couldn't help that the corners of my mouth were starting to climb upwards and Meg raised a hand in defeat.

"Don't play that crap with me, Pippa Winters. I will hit the side of your head so hard I'll make you deaf."

"Sorry, what?" I teased, cupping my right ear toward her and ducking when she threw a playful punch in my direction.

We settled back against our chairs, beers in our hand, looking out onto the ocean. We both had our feet up on chairs to the sides of us, each sporting running sneakers and yoga pants. The winds were picking up and a few salt-and-pepper colored clouds lingered along the skyline.

"It has been a long time, Pippa," Meg said finally. Rust-colored hair dangled at her face as she brushed a piece back behind her ear.

"Since I had something to look forward to?" I teased. My throat tightened when I said the words out loud and I was thankful Meg was on the receiving end of my emotions just then.

"Yes," she said, putting her hand on top of mine and squeezing it.

I nodded.

"Oh, here comes Susan," Meg whispered, eyeing the tray of food headed in our direction. She sat upright and smoothed her hair back, ready to play. Susan sat the tray down and flicked Meg's hand when she tried to take her plate prematurely. "Oh come on Susan, don't make me fight you," Meg bantered.

"Do you fight better before or after you visit the porcelain throne? Just wondering how many more beers it'll take to get you out of my restaurant."

"I'm never leaving," Meg cooed, handing over her empty beer bottle and puckering her lips, blowing air-kisses in her direction.

Susan put both plates in front of us and sighed. "Good," she said, smiling as she walked away with the empty tray.

"Such a love-hate relationship," I said, rolling my eyes.

"Mostly love. She's just mad I've been drinking at this bar since I was eighteen and no one was the wiser."

"What's this?" I asked, eyeing a glass cylinder the size of a penny strategically placed amongst my food. "Some kind of new spice?"

Meg outstretched a hand and I gave it to her, watching her study it. "Looks like a vial of...sand?" she guessed, handing it back.

"A vial of sand? Why? 'Cause there isn't enough sand everywhere else that we need it on our lunch plates?"

"Maybe Susan figured since you're too busy to get to the beach yourself lately, she'd bring the beach to you."

"Maybe I hate you," I offered.

"Negative, you love me. And you're going to share some of those wings with me, too."

"Nope," I responded. "Go swim in the ocean with the sharks, I'm over you."

We ate in silence for a few minutes, glancing between the ocean, the odd vial of sand on my plate, and our disturbingly similar outfits.

"We're damaged, aren't we?" I said finally.

"Oh, most definitely," Meg agreed, stealing a chicken wing off of my plate.

I would have slapped her hand away but my phone rang, so I wiped my fingers across a napkin before pulling my phone from my clutch.

"Work?" Meg questioned, reading my face as a name flashed across the screen.

"The nursing home," I replied, pushing my plate away and standing up. I didn't need to explain anything.

Meg waved me away, not looking up as she slid my plate in front of her. "Your loss, my gain. Go, I got the check," she said.

I nodded, pressing the phone to my ear as I made my way to my car.

Chapter 3

An hour-long car ride to a nursing home can do one of two things when you're worried. It can steamroll every thought and emotion into worst-case scenarios or it can block them out entirely as you autopilot to your location.

I traveled on autopilot most times.

It was a heartless thing to admit to, but when someone's health deteriorates as quickly as I had witnessed, you tend to stop believing that any part of them is still the person you once knew.

My heart was dismembered structurally, slowly, and over time with each visit—I was preparing myself. I was hoping when the loss finally happened, it would soften the blow so my world didn't crumble to my feet all at once.

At least that's what I told myself.

When moments of lucidity happened—unexplained flickers of the person I once knew shined through—it was all the convincing I needed to remember just how hard it would be to let go.

"She's lucid," the nurse at the front desk gushed. "We wanted to be sure before we called you but she's asking for you."

I set my keys on the counter, listening to the metal scrape against the wood, the wide-eyed nurse bursting with questions.

"A year ago," I said finally.

"Excuse me, Ma'm?"

"The last time she was lucid was over a year ago. You're new here and you wouldn't know that but your eyes are begging to know when last time this happened."

"Oh, I'm sorry. I can't imagine..."

I nodded. "Can I see my mom now?"

"Of course!" the nurse exclaimed, waving me away from the sign-in sheet. "Do this later, go see her while she..." Trailing off, her face turned into a crimson canvas and I smiled to ease her embarrassment.

"Go see her while she still remembers me," I said. "I know. Thank you."

My hand hovered above the doorknob to her room as I stood out in the hallway. Trying to remember our last conversation was like trying to recite the exact wording of what I told a patient's family every time I had to explain a permanent mental health diagnosis.

Impossible.

I didn't know it would be our last conversation when it was happening, so I didn't soak up the words to save for a memory. It wouldn't be until later that I wished I could recall exactly what was said, suffocating at the idea that I made her feel anything less than what she truly meant to me.

Cloudiness cycled over and over again in my brain, meshing 'not knowing' with other happier moments I would never forget. It allowed for a balanced spectrum of memories.

I imagined my mom's memories were a paralyzed moment of time that had no counterbalance—if memories existed at all. For that reason alone, I hoped she remembered me on a loop of happier times and not moments like when I sat in the doctor's office holding her hand when she was first diagnosed with early-onset Alzheimer's. I wanted her memories to never repeat the day I had her admitted to a nursing home when her dementia became more than I could handle.

"Pip?"

I turned my head to see Dylan walking down the hall, one hand shoved in his pocket, something he did since they trembled when he was nervous. "What happened, everything okay?"

"What are you—" I started, suddenly shaking my head. "Oh, they call everyone on the emergency list when something like this happens. I forgot to remove you, I'm sorry."

"It's okay, they never took me off since we...?" He shook his head to dismiss the idea of talking about our break up and kissed my forehead once he reached me instead. "Have you gone inside yet? They said she was lucid, I didn't think that was possible anymore."

I turned my gaze back to the doorknob, sighing. "Not yet."

He put his hand over mine, both of us standing motionless, resting against the cold knob. "When you jump, I jump," he whispered. "If you want me here at all."

I nodded, needing him more than I wanted to at that exact moment. My heart raced as I pushed the door open.

She was sitting up in her bed, a book propped in her lap. The room was tidied up—no doubt something she had done while she was aware of where she was. Cleaning when she was anxious was something I had inherited from her. I wondered if she had cried when the nurses first told her that she was in a nursing home and that they would call her daughter. I wondered if she tried to leave.

She smiled when her emerald eyes met mine. Dylan nudged me from behind and I sucked in a breath of air, unsure of what to expect. Putting her book down she outstretched one hand, using the other to cover her mouth as a tear slid down her cheek. "Oh, come here you," she said, patting the bed beside her.

My shoulders loosened as I realized she didn't hate me. "I can't believe I can talk to you again," I said, approaching her bed and settling down next to her.

She cupped my cheek in her hand, "I can't believe it either. How long have I been out? The nurses wouldn't say until you got here."

"Too long," I responded, wiping my own tears away. "You can ask me anything."

"No need, I think it's pretty obvious what happened."

"It is?" I asked, holding her hand in mine and eyeing Dylan.

She laughed, "Well why else would I be wearing these?" Reaching across her stomach she grabbed the corner of the comforter and flipped it off of her, revealing a nightgown and her favorite pair of running sneakers secured to her feet. "They tried to make me take them off but I figured you would get a good laugh at it."

"A good laugh at what, Mom?" I asked, genuinely confused. Dylan shrugged when I looked at him, both of us wondering what we were missing.

"Well clearly I was running and had a fall," she said. "I don't know where I was going but I'm sure glad they were able to get a hold of you to come get me. Can I get discharged now?"

The number of marathons my mother ran throughout her lifetime surpassed anyone I ever knew. She had lived in her running sneakers, taking advantage of every opportunity to train whenever she could. When I was thirteen she bought us matching Nikes that I swore were the reason I won my first track meet in middle school. I wore them until the soles were flatter than pancakes. They were still in a shoebox at the top of my closet.

Most people were proud of the first pair of baby shoes their kids wore. My mother cherished my first pair of running sneakers, since they introduced me to a world she had loved her whole life. We argued through my teenage years due to personality differences—she had an intangible talent of keeping the house spotless and I never wanted to learn to cook anything more than a grilled cheese—but we always came back to running, the one thing that tied our souls together.

"Mom, where do you think you are?" I asked, swallowing hard.

She rolled her eyes. "The hospital of course, why else would I have nurses running in here every few minutes asking who I was? I know who I am, I'm just not sure how long I've been out since *clearly* I hit my head. I don't have the slightest idea what marathon I was training so hard for."

She rubbed her fingers along her hairline looking for a gash that would never exist, squinting to try and remember. Looking past my shoulder she eyed Dylan and smiled. "Roger, love, when did you come home? Did you dye your hair?"

"Roger? Wait, who am I?" I demanded, before he could answer.

"What do you mean? I could never forget who you are," Mom replied.

"Say my name."

"Pippa..." she said, patting my hand in assurance. "I will always know who you are."

"Your daughter or your sister?" I asked.

The silence that followed answered my question. Confusion swirled around the green in her eyes and I could tell that in that moment she became scared.

"I don't have a daughter, Pippa. You know Roger and I didn't work out and I left him when he took the job in Cambodia."

I closed my eyes, frustrated that she could remember her ex-lover but not her own daughter. "Mom, it's me. It's your *daughter* Pippa. You named me after your sister because she died in a car wreck just before I was born. You left Roger, that's true, but you also found out you were two months pregnant soon after he left."

The smile faded from her face and she looked out the window. Dylan shifted his weight behind me and I could hear him clear his throat. When the words never found his lips, he cleared his throat again for good measure and jammed both hands into his pockets.

"Mom, please remember me for just a minute," I begged.

I had seen baby pictures of my Aunt Pippa, and sifted through memory boxes of her from when she was in high school and college. We looked virtually identical, with the only difference being my auburn-colored hair against her dirty blonde. I realized that my new hair color probably complicated things for her more than usual, but the nurses had said she was lucid.

I missed it.

They should have called me sooner.

If the nursing home was only a little closer to where I had been having lunch with Meg...

"Pippa, I'm scared. Where's Roger? Why am I here?"

I nodded at her, fighting to find my voice and to keep the tears at bay so I didn't capsize our visit. "It's okay, I'm here," I assured her. "Everyone's just fine."

I looked around her room, looking for evidence that she had left me a note or letter, but the only things in sight were her photographs and knick-knacks from marathons she had run so many years ago.

After sitting with my mom for a while, posing as her sister, I said goodbye and promised to visit soon. The nurses at the front desk apologized over and over as I signed the visitor log. "It's okay, really," I said. "It probably would have made it harder to say goodbye again."

"She told you about the sand though?" the nurse asked.

"The sand?"

"It's all she will talk about sometimes. When she gets upset the sand in this vial seems to be the only thing that will calm her down lately. We thought maybe she'd tell you where it was from before she..." Her voice trailed off and she looked down the hallway toward her room. "In case when you got here she wasn't..."

I covered my mouth, emotions that I had bottled up while inside her room rising to the surface in vengeance. Dylan's fingers interlocked between mine in response.

"Here." The nurse outstretched a closed fist and I lifted my free hand to meet hers. She deposited a glass cylinder filled with sand in the cusp of my palm.

"Does it mean anything? It seems important," she asked.

I eyed the vial, remembering the one Meg and I had studied at lunch earlier that day. "Yes, it must be but...how is this possible?"

"What is it? Who gave it to her?" Dylan asked, pushing it around in my hand.

"I have no idea," I admitted, wondering who had given me a similar one at The Inlet hours earlier.

Chapter 4

"I don't know why I ever agree to this," Meg huffed, barely able to hoist the weights onto the squat rack. She secured the one side, then collapsed to the floor, stretching her arms above her head and moaning.

"You're so dramatic," I teased.

"I'm not the one trying to kill me."

"You wouldn't be dying if you showed up more than once a month," I replied, joining her on the floor to grab a swig from my water bottle.

The gym was eerily quiet on Wednesday afternoons. People who had a predisposition to binge over the weekend would hit the gym hard at the beginning of the week. Those who had plans for the upcoming weekend would show up at the tail end and turn into weekend warriors until Sunday. Wednesday was like the cousin no one wanted to talk to at the family reunion and avoided by everyone. There was rarely more than a handful of people perusing around in the middle of the day, but it was just the way I liked it. Meg joined me sometimes, but only if I promised to grab an early dinner with her afterward. She wanted to devour her loaded French fries and beer guilt-free. She was naturally agile though, and didn't need nearly as much maintenance as I did since graduating college.

"I can eat more than you," Meg stated.

"And I can bench more than you," I shot back.

"You can," Meg said, nodding. "If I didn't know any better I'd say you were working out more than usual to maintain a certain *physique* for a certain *someone*."

"Nope."

"No one, huh?" Meg raised an eyebrow to impressive new heights.

"No."

"Not even one little swipe right on the Tinder app?" She flicked her pointer finger in my direction.

"Nothing."

"No sneaking into room two-thirty-three late at night in your scrubs?"

"Room two-thirty—? Hey! How'd you know about him?"

"Ah HA, so there IS someone!"

"There is not, I just have no idea how you knew about that guy," I said.

"Morgan told me."

"Morgan?"

"Yep," Meg said, looking at her fingernails.

"Who the hell is Morgan?"

She put down her hand, a devilish grin spreading across her face. "First name Captain..."

"Ohhhh of course, you took advantage of my brain when I was drinking." I sat up on the cool mat beneath me, pinching the space between my nose and trying not to snort from laughing so hard. "You jerk."

"Morgan knows *all* things," Meg said, opening her arms wide and staring up at the oversized fan wobbling in circles above us. "So two-thirty-three *wasn't* your patient...?"

"No..."

"But you treated him anyway?"

"I'm not getting into this."

"Is that legal? Don't you have designated patients for a reason? I think I need to speak to your supervisor."

"There's no rule about being friendly to someone or checking in on a patient to go above and beyond when you know your boss happens to be wandering the halls."

"So this was a one time thing?"

"It wasn't a thing!" I said

"Seems like a thing," Meg said, shrugging. "According to Morgan, he seemed like the *only* thing."

"Well Morgan and I are no longer friends then," I said.

"Fair enough," Meg said, putting her right leg out in front of her to stretch. "You really don't see him anymore?"

"I really don't."

"Because you don't want to or...?"

"He was discharged," I said, catching the hint of sadness in my own voice. "And it happened when I wasn't on shift so—"

"Ohhh! You didn't even get to say goodbye!" Meg said, cutting me off and tilting her head with empathy. "Do you know his last name? Maybe we could—"

"Meg, no..."

"I'm so good at finding people though. This one time, I tracked this guy on Instagram who—"

"Meg!"

We sat there in silence for a moment, listening to the hum of the cooler behind the reception area and the distant grunting of a man trying to deadlift more than he should somewhere in the back of the gym.

"I don't know how you do it," Meg said softly. "How you can treat people who have been in the military."

"They're just like anyone else," I said.

Meg's eyes were watering before I finished my sentence. "But we both know they're not," she said.

"Oh, Meg, no. I didn't mean...Cheryl was different, she was..."

"Lost," Meg finished. "She was my lost, baby sister and no one could help her find her way back. Not that she didn't try. The Army certainly didn't come running when she told them she was depressed and having anxiety attacks on a daily basis."

"I know," I said. I reached for Meg's hand, but she slowly backed it away.

"Now that I think about it they weren't very fast to show up to the funeral when she overdosed either."

"I know, I know. I'm not sure anyone really knew how bad she was hurting."

"They knew," Meg said, narrowing her eyes. She picked at the laces of her Brooks and sighed, shaking her head. She was literally shaking the thought of her sister out of her head. "Well I'm going to go cycle for a bit and get this adrenaline out. Want to come?"

I knew from the hardened look on her face that she was going to need some time to decompress before she bounced back. "No, you go, I want to run instead so I think I'll go sprint on the beach. I'll meet you back here and we'll go stuff our faces, okay?"

"Deal," Meg said. "Speaking of Cheryl, do you think we can pick up Phoenix on the way? I'm sure she'd love to throw French fries on the floor and put some frozen yogurt up her nose while we eat."

"She's *three* already," I nodding in disbelief. "Of course we can pick her up, I thoroughly enjoy watching you be the coolest aunt in the world to that little ray of sunshine. It makes my ovaries ache and stuff."

"Are they capable of aching? I'm pretty sure your ovaries are old and dried up." Meg pulled herself into a standing position as she continued. "Plus I'm pretty sure a penis has to be involved to like, make a kid. I remember that from anatomy class I think."

"Don't fall off your bike!" I called after her as she walked away, giving me the finger.

A wall of dense, crisp air enveloped my body as I stepped outside the gym. I wrinkled my nose, wondering if maybe I should just run on the treadmill instead. North Carolina had fairly mild winters, which was ideal for training purposes, but it was cooler than I preferred for the middle of February. I decided against it, since the beach was a close three blocks distance. Jogging over with ease, I laced up my sneakers a bit tighter near the water's edge once I made my way down to the surf.

There was a line of condos in various colors parallel to the ocean, so I chose a yellow one off in the distance as my bull's-eye while I stretched. I started a light jog until I reached a blue condo with a wrap around porch, and then sprinted the rest of the way to the yellow condo. Then I'd walk back to my starting point and do it all over.

The beach was deserted. The lone surfers who sometimes braved the waters in wetsuits during the winter months were nowhere to be seen, but sweat trickled down my cheekbones anyway. I adjusted my ear buds, cranking up my music as I made my way back to my starting point for the third time. I was surprised to see a man wearing a gray hoodie stretching his calf muscles a few hundred feet away. He glanced at his watch and appeared to be setting something, then stared out into the ocean again as he grabbed onto his other ankle.

I turned my back to him, grabbing my left ankle for a quick stretch while mentally locking eyes with my goal in the distance. The first few steps I took were interrupted by a spritz of sand shooting across my ankles.

Startled, I glanced to my side and saw the man sprinting beside me. Cautiously, I increased my speed to put some distance between us. The footsteps faded, and I smirked at the ease of pulling ahead so easily. Refocusing my attention to what was in front of me, a gray blur whirled past, kicking sand against my thighs in protest of my previous victory.

"What the—?" I gasped, flailing my arms thinking I was being attacked. The guy in gray barreled ahead, putting several feet between us. "Oh no you don't!"

I re-positioned my body—preparing for full sprint-mode—closing the gap between us each time my feet hit the sand. I maneuvered to his right to get better traction against the hard-packed sand closer to the ocean, hoping to gain an upper hand. He guessed my play, shifting toward the right as I continued to approach. Like a switch, I felt runner's high kick in. "Wooooooo!" I yelled out.

Gray-guy looked over his shoulder just in time to watch me match his pace. We hovered there, our bodies humming in rhythm against the sand and the surf. Passing the yellow condo that was my original target we remained steadfast. Our rhythm hiccupped momentarily, and I started to pull out ahead of him.

"Wait!" the guy shouted, a muffled cry against the music beating through my ear buds.

I ignored him, even more convinced to push forward at his cries of defeat.

"Wait!"

The basketball-sized dimple of sand came out of no where. The sudden hump caught the front part of my toe, sending me flying forward. Just before I hit the ground my body was shielded, a firm hand encased around my head as we tuck-and-rolled to a stop.

"I told you to wait!" the guy said. His head was lowered, the hood from his sweatshirt drooping to my chest. He was panting like a cheetah that lost his kill.

"I just thought you were being a sore loser," I admitted, pulling one ear bud out.

"I didn't know we were racing."

"You started it, I was just doing intervals when you went all Boston Marathon on me."

He raised his head, an amused twist on the only part of his mouth I could see. He pushed the hood from his face, huffing. "What can I say, I run better when I have a challenge."

I opened my mouth in shock, my heart crashing against my chest like the waves surrounding us. "Two-thirty-three? Is that you?" I could barely get the words out, looking over his shoulder to see if I was on some kind of candid camera.

"Two-thirty-three?" He looked confused. "Is that an agent thing? Are you F.B.I?" he asked, only half-serious.

"No, I'm— I'm sorry it's just that I think we know each... I think we've met. Right?" I treaded water lightly. Sometimes the patients we treated were so distraught or pumped full of meds that they weren't able to remember the majority of their hospital stay. Since I technically wasn't assigned to his room when he was admitted, I wanted to see if he had recognized *me* first. I had been drawn to him while he was under our care, needing to check in on him even when I didn't know why myself.

Then, after the time limit for his psychiatric hold expired, he was gone.

A haze of curiosity reflected from his hazel eyes as he stared at me. His gaze skimmed down my nose, resting on my lips. He parted his, sucking in a breath and I braced myself for him to out me about sneaking into his room during non-visiting hours for nonsense reasons. I brought him a cup of water twelve times, replaced his tissue box like he had brain matter dripping from his nose, and swapped out glove boxes just to have one more chance to speak with him.

"Yeah," he said, slowly nodding his head. "Yeah, I have no idea."

"Oh!" I said with way too much enthusiasm, "Must be someone else then."

He nodded, his hand still cupped behind my hair acting like a barrier to the sand. "Can I ask you something?" The seriousness of his eyes ignited the fragments of emotion I felt when visiting him. He lowered his chin, and the anticipation of whether or not he was going to kiss me was overpowering.

"Yes," I said, watching his gaze start to glow in the winter sunset.

"Did you make a train noise?"

"What?"

"A train noise. Did you...you know, make a noise like a train when you were running?"

My cheeks flushed. "What? No! Why would I make a train noise?"

32

"Well, your cheeks right now are telling me you did."

"That wouldn't even make sense."

"It doesn't, that's why I was asking if you did. I could have sworn you were reenacting Thomas the Train back there."

His stupid half-grin snapped me back to reality. "I did not, how would you know what noises I make?"

He pointed to the side of his head. "No headphones."

"You don't run with music?"

"No, it's distracting."

"So are you. You can get up now."

Realizing we were still pressed against each other his eyes widened in embarrassment, then softened. "Why, is a train coming?"

"Oh just—" I pushed against his shoulder, trying not to let him see me laughing as I stood up and brushed myself off.

When I turned to face him I was taken aback by his height. Watching him brush the remnants of sand from his shorts, combing his hand through his hair, and looking out into the distance I couldn't think of a time he'd ever looked so healthy, so self-reliant.

Then he looked at me.

His eyes told a completely different story. They contained a depth that pulled me in, but a force field that warned I shouldn't get too close.

"I'm going to need your number now," he said.

"What for?"

"Dinner, of course. I can't let the winner of the race go home empty-handed. I think dinner would be perfect. Aren't you starving after runs like that?"

"I like to eat," I admitted.

"So, we're on for tonight?" He traced over my face, watching me pause for a second too long. "Oh, you have plans already?"

"I do," I said, my voice weighing heavier than I expected it to. "What would your consolation prize be?"

"You'll be there at dinner, right?" he asked, handing me a phone from his pocket so I could enter in my number.

I hesitated. I knew that doctor-patient relationships had a code of ethics a mile long that had to be upheld. Peering down the coastline I considered the possibility that at one point he might want someone to talk to, someone to encourage him to go back to the hospital again. Since he wasn't technically a patient anymore, and we technically met on the beach having a friendly race, I didn't see the harm. He nudged the phone toward me, raising an eyebrow in a way that forced me to smile.

I took it.

I punched in my number, returning it to him as he read the screen. "Nice to meet you, Pippa. I'll text you so you have my number too." He touched the screen a few times, and returned the phone to his pocket just as the phone in my pocket chimed. "So, since you gave me your actual number, not a dummy one, I'm assuming it's okay we chat and figure out when dinner can be?"

I shrugged, trying to mask my grin, "Guess so."

"By the way, I'm Jackson," he said, walking backwards. He raised his eyebrows, then turned on his heel to run off into the sunset.

"I know," I whispered behind him.

Chapter 5

Jackson never called.

He never texted or tried to find me on the plethora of social media sites I was sure we both frequented. I tried to not let it bother me, especially knowing the past of how we really met. Considering how destitute he was in the hospital, I was worried there was a different, more compelling reason he didn't reach out other than no longer having an interest in dinner.

I wanted him to be okay. At least when he was hospitalized I was able to check in on him whenever he crossed my mind.

Meg picked up on the residual flirty hangover emitting from my smile when I met her back at the gym that day. I had to dish on how a random, albeit easy on the eyes, man tried to run me down on the beach and how we might revisit my Olympic games victory over dinner. I excluded mentioning that he had been the same man from the hospital who had been my fake-patient or that he was the identity behind door two-thirty-three.

She immediately dismissed my comment about the aesthetics of his face, telling me that my definition of guy-throbs was slightly off Richter ever since college.

We parted ways after dinner and Meg spent the better part of the next two days harassing me about every single bachelor she could, reveling that she felt my 'dating switch' had been turned back on.

"If you want to see someone *really* easy on the eyes, you need to come visit me at work right now," Meg hissed into the phone.

"You're just trying to get me to come to The Inlet on my day off to day-drink. I should do the responsible thing and go home to sleep and then, oh I don't know, go for a ten mile run or something."

"Yes, exactly, you need to day-drink. You've been training too hard lately anyway. Come see this guy though, just for a few minutes. I'm going to talk you up before you get here. He'll have no choice but to propose to you the second you walk in the door."

"Please don't."

"Blind date, Inlet style."

"You're a terrible person. I thought you don't call customers from the bar? Isn't that your golden rule? No playing Cupid while you bartend, no matter how much the customer is crying on your bar?"

"My bar, my call. You'll thank me, trust. See ya in five," she said, hanging up.

I pulled into the parking lot of The Inlet, not attempting to fix my ponytail before heading inside. "Sorry, Prince Charming," I said out loud, putting my car in park. "I'm too tired to play dress-up today."

Meg was behind the bar, her high-profile bun bobbing all over as she fake-laughed to something a guy sitting at the bar whispered. I sighed, spotting the guy from the back and immediately regretting my decision to show up. I looked around, wondering if I could sneak back out before she noticed.

"Hey, girlfriend! Hey!" Meg waved with just the tips of her fingers, motioning me over. "Come have a drink, beautiful."

The guy peered over his shoulder as I approached and I wondered what planet Meg was living on by calling me. Sitting on a stool next to my prearranged suitor, I spoke to Meg directly, not knowing if I could muster the strength to not speak through gritted teeth. "Hi friend," I cooed, tilting my head to the side, widening my eyes.

A cheeky, full tooth smile was my reply. "What's your drink, lady?"

I looked at the guy, mulling him over. If Meg and I were out at a bar and he approached us I wouldn't deny a drink if he offered, but I certainly wouldn't consider going home with him. He was wearing work boots, which was a good sign, at least he had a job. Most of his hair was still there, except for a small circular patch at the back of his head he probably wasn't aware of. Blond hair, so he still had at least a decade before he'd have to shave it off. Squinting, I tried to see where Meg could possibly—

"Ay, love, can I have me another?" he said.

Ah, there it was.

I smirked, raising approving eyebrows at Meg as she approached him with a fresh beer, absorbing the Irish accent and relaxing knowing she knew me so well. I was a sucker for a foreign accent.

"Thought maybe you'd want a Long Island," she said, pushing it in my direction, winking.

"Go strong or go home, got it," I replied, then lowered my voice. "He's okay." I ticked my head in his direction. "What's his name?"

She looked around, landing her eyes on the guy beside me, whispering just as carefully. "Who? Connor?"

The guy looked up at the sound of his name. "What's that, love?"

"Oh nothing, you're good," Meg replied, flashing another fake smile until he returned to his beer. She turned to me, her voice barely audible. "Connor's the new cook. I made Susan hire him last week."

"They didn't need another cook."

"I know that. But the *accent.*" She gripped the edge of the bar, biting her lip.

Connor finished the last of his beer and wiped his face, pushing his chair away from the bar and heading toward the double doors to the kitchen.

"How'd you get Susan to sign off on that one?" I asked, genuinely impressed. "And is he supposed to be drinking while on the clock?"

"Told her I'd quit. And he wasn't drinking on the clock, he just clocked in now."

"Mature."

"Desperate times call for desperate measures. I don't want to sleep with him, I just want him to talk dirty to me."

"Oh, Meg!" I said, covering my nose to hide an impending snort.

"Ay, love, want me to cook your potatoes?" Meg said, impersonating his Irish accent.

I turned my face to the side, hiding the giggles.

"Want me to show you how to chug a Guinness?" she continued, forcing both eyebrows to do the wave while she smiled.

The chair moved to the left of me and a gruff, "Seat taken?" broke our laughter.

"No you're good," I said, wiping my eyes and looking up so I could gauge whether the person had enough room to squeeze next to me.

"Jackson!" I said, all laughter ceasing to exist.

"Wait you know him?" Meg said, pointing her finger at his face.

"You could say that," Jackson said. "Would you mind grabbing my beer from the other end of the bar, Meg?" Then he lowered his voice, "Didn't realize I'd have competition this early in the day," he said, nodding in the direction Connor had disappeared.

"Pippa, this is Jackson," Meg said through clenched teeth. "Apparently you already knew that, so I guess I didn't have to hold him hostage with fun facts about you while we waited for you to get here."

"*THIS* is who you wanted me to meet? Oh, you didn't..." I begged, realizing what she had said.

"Oh, but she did," Jackson answered lightly, tilting the beer to his lips as Meg handed it to him. "I know lots about you now, Pippa Winters."

"You told him my last name!"

"She told me your last name," he repeated, keeping his straight face and laughing eyes.

"Meg!"

"What?! How was I supposed to know you two had already met? And why don't you know *his* last name then?" she asked.

"Yeah what's your last name?" I demanded, even though I had seen it on his medical charts numerous times.

Amused, he obliged. "Walker."

"Ohhhhhh, I love it," Meg gushed, resting her elbows on the counter and plopping her chin in her hands.

"His last name?" I questioned, eyeing her suspiciously.

She shook her shoulders, a pretend shiver traveling from her head to her tailbone. "Men who have verbs as last names. It's so sexy."

There was a silent moment where Jackson and I exchanged glances incredulously, the comment almost too ripe to respond to.

Meg took a step back as the first bout of laughter roared out of Jackson. Taking her by surprise, she retreated to the back end of the bar, staring at him like he was a caged animal that had just been let loose.

My laughter started with a choked snort. Hot tears stung the inner corner of my eyes where day-old mascara started to puddle off.

Jackson covered his mouth as he laughed and I wondered if he had learned that behavior from having braces when he was younger. He certainly didn't need to hide his smile now; it lit up a room as quickly as efficiently as his eyes darkened it.

Jackson's pointer finger and thumb were suddenly on my lower back, his head bent over the bar in a fit of laughter that he couldn't overcome.

The subtle, innocent gesture made me stop laughing, and I struggled to change the subject as Meg eyed my reaction. "Okay Chuckles, it's not that funny."

"Yeah, yeah it is because that's not even the best part of—," a genuine squeak of new laughter bubbled from his mouth and he couldn't finish his sentence.

"Someone has a good sense of humor," Meg said awkwardly.

"I'm a verb, but you're a train!" Jackson said, covering his mouth and gasping into the cusp.

My eyebrows came together, "I'm a—? OH MEG, YOU DIDN'T!" I yelled.

Meg stepped backwards with her hands in a surrender pose, realizing she had been dishing dirty secrets to someone I already knew. "I'm a bad friend, I'm a bad friend," she chanted.

Jackson pointed to Meg, wiping his eyes and taking a huge gulp of air. "She told me when you were in college you'd get a really intense runner's high and would yell out like a train whistle during track meets. I knew it, I knew you made a train noise the other day on the beach."

Meg cringed listening to Jackson throw her under the bus. Immediately upon absorbing the last of his comment though, her eyes widened and she pointed at me with such haste I thought her earrings were going to rock right out of her earlobes. "HE'S THE GUY FROM THE BEACH?"

"Guilty," Jackson said, raising his glass and downing the rest of his beer. He wiped the outer edge of his left eye, sighing as he finally caught his breath.

"I don't want to hear it," I warned, narrowing my eyes at her. "Any other tidbits you mentioned that I should know about?"

"Just that you're waiting to see if you've qualified for the Boston Marathon," Jackson answered for her. "Now I know why you're so competitive."

"Meghan!" I said, genuinely hurt.

Meg covered her eyes. "Oh, you used my whole first name. I'm the worst best friend, I'm the worst, I know it. I'll never speak to you again. I don't deserve you in my life."

"So, he knows about Dylan then?" I said, throwing one hand in the air while I sucked back the remainder of my Long Island with the other waiting for her response.

"Oh no, no Pippa," Meg said, glancing at Jackson. "I would never…"

"Who's Dylan?" Jackson asked, all giggle-bugs firmly at bay.

"He's none of your business," I said, eyeing Meg, coaxing her to keep quiet.

"More drinks?" Meg asked, eyeing the empty ones in front of us. "I think everyone could use more drinks. I'd certainly like a drink."

"I'm not done with you," I threatened as she walked away.

"So, Boston huh?" Jackson started.

"Drop it."

"Nah, I get it, you don't want to tell anyone just in case you don't qualify. It's cool."

I sucked in a balloon's worth of air, ready to rant about how he knew nothing about me when he continued.

"So, let's train together."

"Huh? Why?"

"Clearly we're good motivators for each other."

"I have my own motivations, thanks."

"Yeah, but none like me."

I opened my mouth but nothing came out. Meg returned with two beers this time, handing one to each of us. "You guys look cozy so I'm just gonna..." she pointed to the end of the bar where a twenty-something brunette had just sat down.

"Thanks, but no thanks," I said, watching Meg slink away. "I'm perfectly capable of training on my own."

"What's your best time?" he asked.

"None of your business."

"Yep, you need me."

"Why's that?"

"If you didn't, if you were proud of the time you have, you'd have told me. Since you didn't that tells me you're struggling to push yourself to your full potential."

"Oh, so we're a psychoanalyst now are we?" I teased.

"No, are you?" he asked.

"I—uh, well, what do I do for work, you mean?"

Jackson smirked as his pocket vibrated, a call distracting him at just the right moment.

"Tell you what," he said, clicking the edge of his phone to send the call to voicemail. "Drink your beer faster than me and I'll leave it alone." He waved his hand over the bar to visually demonstrate he

41

would cease provoking me. "If I finish first though, you have to let me train you for your marathon."

"What do you know about running in marathons?"

"Nothing," he said. "I know everything about body conditioning though, and you'd be amazed at what I could show you."

"So you'll call me then? Just like you did last time to set up our pretend dinner date?"

"No, I'll show up. When it matters, I'm there. I'll show up for you." He raised his beer, nudging at the air to get me to do the same. "Here's to Boston then?"

My hand was wrapped around my glass, the buzz from my previous drink finally hitting me and making me more agreeable than I would have been otherwise.

"Yeah, I don't know Jackson. I don't even know if I qualified yet, and you just don't seem like the kind of guy who—." I had two gulps in before Jackson realized what was happening, a panicked look painting his face.

"Hey! What the—!" He tipped his drink back, wasting no time in leveling the playing field, both of us racing to the bottom of our glasses.

"Go Jackson!" Meg yelled from across the bar.

I eyed her angrily over my glass and she changed teams. "Pippa! Yeah go, Pippa!" she called out, less enthused.

Glass clinked against the counter top, with a victorious Jackson smiling and wiping his mouth with the back of his hand. "*AND* you cheated!" he said, pointing to the last gulp in my glass.

"Ugh," I said, abandoning the last gulp at the bottom. "How'd you do that so fast?"

"Practice, just like how we're going to practice to make you the fastest you can be by race day," he said, reaching into his pocket as his phone vibrated again.

"Ah, I should take this," he said, pushing his stool from the bar. He maneuvered his way to the outside deck, scraping his work boots against the floor and running his hand down the length of his shirt to rid it of the condensation that had been transferred from his beer glass.

"He's hot," Meg said behind me.

I jumped. "Hi friend, didn't see you there."

"I know," Meg said, winking. "Your gaze was busy on other thinnnnnngs."

"He's okay."

"Like I said, you never were very good at determining who was or wasn't easy on the eyes. I am *telling* you he is."

Trying not to make it obvious, I watched Jackson in my peripherals. He pulled the phone away from his ear and stared at the screen for a brief moment before returning it to his pocket, shaking his head in disgust. He stuffed both hands in his pockets then, staring out onto the ocean. A breeze rustled his t-shirt and I could almost smell his cologne wafting into the bar. He remained solidified to the deck, unmoving. Thinking there was a chance he wasn't coming back inside, I pushed my stool away from the bar to make my way toward him.

I stood next to him for a solid minute, rubbing my arms in the chilly breeze and watching his gaze hover over the ocean in front of us. He wasn't staring at anything in particular, but everything at the same time. A hollow, befuddled expression filled his eyes and I shuddered. Part of me wanted to go back inside, the silence between us deafening. Instead, I wondered if he just needed...

His reflexes were astonishing. My wrist was clenched in his grasp almost the instant I touched his shoulder. I didn't mean to yell out, and I could see Meg running out from behind the bar. Jackson's breaths were shallow, forced, and he looked at my hand like it was a grenade.

"We're okay, Meg," I said, keeping my voice level as she approached, my eyes locked on Jackson's face.

"Pip?" she questioned, approaching us like she was stepping over eggshells on the floor.

"We're good, right Jackson?" I asked.

He blinked at me, the laughing, full-of-life Jackson nowhere to be found. He nodded, robotic movements answering the question.

"Meg, we're going to walk off the deck and onto the beach for a minute."

"Pip, I don't think—"

"Come on, Jackson. Walk with me."

At first he stood motionless as I slowly uncurled his fingers from around my wrist. They had already begun to bruise but I didn't bring it to his attention. The sand was just off the deck, and I was thankful it was mid-day. There was barely anyone inside, never mind out on the deck to watch us. I guided him to the sand, offering my other palm for him to take. He did, and the sensation of my fingers intertwined with his caused him to look down at his hand.

"Sit with me," I said. Gently bending my knees, I lowered myself to the beach and sat in the frigid sand, grabbing a handful.

Jackson complied, bending his knees. He faltered for a moment as he crouched down, sitting with me.

"Open your hand," I said. He did, and I put the sand into his palm, pulling his fingers apart to let it sift through the gaps like a waterfall. "You feel that?" I asked, gauging his responsiveness.

"Again?" he asked, opening his palm but staring past me. I nodded, breathing a little easier as the color returned to his face and the clenched fist of his other hand relaxed.

After sifting the sand through his fingers two more times, I eased back into conversation. "I didn't mean to startle you, Jackson. I shouldn't have touched your shoulder like that."

"When did you touch me?" he asked. When his eyes met mine they were genuinely afraid.

I didn't answer.

"Pippa, did I do something? Did I—?" He looked me over, looking for any obvious signs he had hurt me.

"You kids okay out here?" Meg yelled, interrupting from the deck.

"We were just talking, everything's good. We'll be back inside in a minute."

"Meg," Jackson called out, staring at me with the softest eyes I've ever seen. "Get me my check, please."

Meg didn't ask questions as we both paid our tabs and walked to the parking lot. Neither of us said anything, and we lingered by our cars for an awkward amount of time not knowing how to fill the silence.

"So you'll call me?"

"Hmmm..." he said, half-aware of why he would do such a thing. He nodded, taking a deep breath. "Oh yeah, the marathon. Boston. Yeah, I'll call then."

"Not just for that," I said, moving toward him. An invisible tether pulled me in his direction, and I made sure his eyes weren't off in the distance when I reached for his hand. "Anytime you want to," I assured, my hand brushing the top of his.

He looked down, his fingers twitching to fight off the urge to take my hand. Forcing a smile he nodded again. Then he turned to open his door, starting the engine once he was inside.

Adrenaline had sobered me up and I found myself headed home instead of back into the bar to talk to Meg.

Pulling up to my house I stopped to grab the mail before heading inside, flicking through letters as a distraction.

That's when I saw it.

"I made it," I whispered, reading over the acceptance letter after ripping it open. Punching the air I grabbed my phone, tapping the screen like a lunatic to tell Meg that I was officially a qualified runner for the Boston Marathon.

I locked my phone and set it down on the counter, smiling like a buffoon. My smile faded as I thought about who I wanted to tell next, Jackson popping into my head unannounced.

Opening my phone I slid through my messages and found his name, scanning the only text he had sent me:

Hey it's Jackson, you'll remember
me as the guy who lost the beach race. Dinner?

I sighed, remembering his breath on my lips and the way he cradled my head just before I hit the ground.

45

Jackson had hit the ground at The Inlet, I watched it happen, and I didn't see the signs before he fell.

"Just ask if he's okay," I said out loud. Starting to type, I filled up the spot to reply and tell him he'd better prepare to train me just to start off the conversation.

Almost as if in direct response, three gray dots bubbled up on the bottom of the screen when I was mid-sentence, indicating that Jackson was writing something at the same time.

I held my breath as the bubbles danced across the screen in a lazy rhythm. After a moment passed I wondered if he was typing something lengthy or typing and deleting what he was saying.

Then, they stopped.

I stared at the screen for a full three minutes, waiting for the bubbles to reappear.

They never did.

I deleted what I wrote and stared a while longer. Locking my phone I pushed it away from me on the counter, burying my head in my hands.

Curiosity consumed me, wanting to know why he never pushed send.

All he managed to give me were three gray dots.

Chapter 6

"If you don't mind me asking, how did your parents die?" I was flat on my back staring up at the sky, grabbing onto my left shin and pulling my knee to my belly to get a deeper stretch.

Jackson stood facing the waves, his right foot in his hand as he teeter-tottered to gain balance and stretch his thigh. ""You were twenty minutes late and you want to start out with that topic?"

"I texted you I was going to be late," I protested.

"You didn't say why."

"I didn't think I needed to, I'm a busy person," I said, wanting him to drop it. "Oh, I mean not that you're *not* busy, I was just saying—"

"They were poisoned."

I sat upright, watching for tells on his face that he was kidding. "What?"

"They were poisoned."

"At the same time?"

Jackson nodded. "At the same time and in the same way."

"Do they know who did it?"

"Their car," he replied, nonchalantly.

I struggled to follow. "How did their car poison them, Jackson?" I put my hands behind me and spread them out into the sand, feeling around with restlessness.

The method of training that Jackson preferred consisted of short bouts of running intervals with gaps of stretching and rest in-between. Normally I'd protest, since the short bursts of two to four miles weren't enough to fully unleash all of the adrenaline I had. One week into training I found myself gravitating in favor of the stretching parts, preferring it to running since it gave us a chance to pause and get to know each other better.

The legs on Jackson were intimidating. He was a workhorse, digging his feet into the ground and connecting like a wire finding its ground. An unlimited stamina harbored inside of him, and at times I felt like I was pushing myself too hard. An injury would ruin everything. Somehow he knew exactly when I was about to max out, slowing down to a trot just as I was trigged with muscle exhaustion.

"Jackson?" I asked again, wondering if he didn't hear my question. "We don't have to talk about it if—"

"They had a luxury car with keyless entry. Quietest motor on the market, they said." He paused, clearing his throat, and lingered a second too long before continuing.

"Oh no..." I said, suddenly seeing through the foggy overtones.

"They were out to dinner one night, and Dad had one too many whiskey sours talking with a client so Mom had to drive home. She wasn't used to driving his car and she left it running in the garage. All night. They never woke up."

I brought my hand to my mouth. "Did *you* find them?"

"I didn't. I was at a neighbor's spending the night since they knew they'd be out late. It was two weeks before I graduated high school so my parents didn't care about a mid-week sleepover. Our housekeeper found them, and we heard her screams from three houses down. I ran home, Mom took the key fob out but forgot to shut the car off. It just looked like they were sleeping in their beds upstairs. I'm sure they didn't feel a thing."

"You went inside?"

"I didn't think twice. I just ran in."

"You could've been killed too."

"I didn't consider it."

"You're lucky you got out of there."

"I can't remember things, sometimes."

"Huh?" I asked, not sure if we were shifting topics to what happened the other day at The Inlet.

"I wouldn't leave their sides until the ambulance got there. I inhaled enough that it impacted my memory, just slightly. You'd never know unless I told you. It wasn't too noticeable at first. Maybe I would forget my jacket before heading home from work or didn't call someone back when I said I would, nothing dangerous. Now..." He trailed off, not wanting to finish the sentence.

Nodding, I wondered how much of his hospital stay was the responsibility of that accident versus his medical charts telling me he was a veteran with PTSD. The lost look on his face that day at The Inlet was painful to see, he truly didn't remember grabbing me and I was willing to bet the majority of his recollection from his hospital stay had also been extinguished.

"That's one hell of a freak accident," I said.

"It's actually way more common than people think. Twenty-eight people died last year from the same thing. There's several lawsuits open but I didn't want to get caught up in that, I wasn't around anyway afterwards."

"So is that what made you join the military? Was your dad a veteran or did you just need to get away?"

He grabbed at his chest as if having a heart attack. "My dad? A veteran? He wouldn't have the grit." The smile dissipated, and he stared at me. "I never said anything about being in the military."

I stammered to find a reply. "Oh? I thought... yeah I could have sworn you mentioned something before."

"I know for a fact I didn't."

He was sitting in the sand by then, hugging his knees. Most of the time we were dressed for chilly weather, so not much was exposed, but the sun had done his complexion a favor. Healthier than I had ever seen him when he was admitted, I stole a look at his arms, which were impressively flexed and being backlit by the sun.

"I guessed," I said, still staring at his arms so I wouldn't be tempted to divert my eyes from his when as I lied.

"You guessed?"

"You're really fit and you keep your hair nice. I'd guess you go at least once a week to have it cut."

"You guessed all that from my haircut?"

"You're disciplined and hold yourself a certain way. Also, you're bossy."

"Am not."

I opened my arms in a look-around-you way. "Yeah you're not bossy at all, yet here we are, training for a marathon you have nothing to do with."

"Kiss me," he replied.

"What?" I looked around, not entirely sure who else I was expecting to see standing around us.

"Why do you look so surprised? I didn't stutter, I said kiss me." He opened his hands, curling his pointer finger in a come-hither motion.

"Jackson...I..."

"What? You don't want to?"

"No!"

"No, you don't want to kiss me?" The corner of his mouth started turning upward and something about it annoyed me. I couldn't tell if he was being serious or mocking me.

"No, I mean yes. I mean no, I didn't say that I would *not* kiss you but..."

"But what?"

"But why?" I demanded.

"'Cause I'm bossy, right? That's what bossy people do, they demand things."

"I don't even know you," I replied. "Come on, tell me something funny about yourself instead."

"Something funny?"

"Yeah, I don't know. Tell me a good story."

He considered it for a minute, looking anywhere but my eyes. "I can't seem to throw my garbage can away."

"Huh?" I asked.

"Yeah I can't throw it away, every time I leave it at the curb for them to take they just think I don't have any garbage for that can. It's annoying, I've been trying to throw it away for months."

My cheeks were pinched upward in laughter for what seemed like forever, and I was pretty sure I snorted just before catching my breath and settling down. "I actually couldn't breathe there for a second," I said, wiping away a tear.

He nodded at the success of his story, bringing his chin into his chest and staring at the sand between his feet. "You're right. I don't know you either. What about your parents?"

I stiffened. "What about them?"

"Well mine are dead, so I don't have much to say about them. You're a woman, yet you never bring up your mother or your father. That tells me you either have a bad relationship with them or they're dead too."

"Great hypothesis," I said, rolling my eyes.

"So they're dead?"

"Not exactly," I replied.

"Enlighten me."

"I don't really know my father so there's not much to tell. He left before I was born. My mom never talked about him much but she never had to, I didn't ask."

"Deadbeat?"

"A higher calling, actually."

"He became a priest?"

"Eh, in a way. He was a doctor and he had the opportunity to travel to the remote village of Roka in western Battambang. Oh, that's in—"

"Cambodia, I'm familiar."

"Excuse *me*," I said, holding up my hands and pushing back an invisible wall of air. *Great, his mind is as beautiful as he is.* "Yeah, well, long story short is he never came back." I held up my palms, shrugging my shoulders. "Too bad, so sad."

"He didn't try to write or come home to visit?"

"He was too busy saving the world, Mom said."

"Sorry to hear that."

"I'm not at all," I replied. "I never met him so there was no connection there and my mom found a really spectacular replacement father for me."

Jackson laughed.

"No really," I said, laughing with him. "He showed up to every dumb school event, every dance. He was everything he didn't have to be."

"Was?"

My laughter faded. "Heart attack."

Jackson nodded, raising his eyebrows. "Always the great ones who go first, huh?"

"Something like that," I said, looking out onto the water, feeling the salty air start to burn the corners of my eyes. "He's a big reason why I got into the medical field. I thought maybe there was a way I could have saved him."

"You're a doctor? You never told me that. Where do you work?"

Busted.

"Not a doctor per say, I'm a registered nurse." I flicked my shoe, hoping he would be satisfied with my answer and gloss over the subject.

"What hospital? Any of the local ones?" He was fishing and I knew I had a split-second choice to make. If I told him the truth now I'd probably never see him again and if I lied I'd be setting up our relationship to sleep in a bed of deception I'd have to address at a later time before he found out.

I needed more time.

"You probably wouldn't know it, it's a smaller hospital out past where my mom is, so it's over an hour from here."

I knew the question about my mother was next and it was a person and topic I only discussed with Meg so I braced myself, gearing to put my guard up.

"Your mom?" he asked gently, reading my face before he asked.

When I looked at Jackson his heart was on his sleeve. He had such an innate way of sensing my feelings just by looking at me and I appreciated it more than I could ever tell him out loud. When a man is perceptive enough to read a woman before *she's* aware of what she feels, you know he's pure. He should be kept, and appreciated and...

It hit me that Jackson had none of those things.

No one kept him. He was a yacht lost at sea, beautiful to look at from afar—so no one would ever consider asking if it were sinking. He was abandoned, drifting alone among a lullaby of waves, waiting for something or someone to find him and bring him home.

"You and my mom would have a lot in common," I said finally.

"She's military?" he asked, impressed.

I shook my head. "She can't remember things sometimes."

Jackson inched closer, facing me, our ankles touching each other in a silent hug. "She can't remember things...sometimes?" he asked, hopeful.

"All the times, actually," I said.

He didn't speak when I looked away, a single tear sliding down my cheek. "She loved the beach. It was her favorite place in the whole world."

"Is she able to do day trips? Get out every once in a while?"

"Never. She's in a home. I wish I could bring the beach to her sometimes," I answered, mumbling the last word with every bit of guilt it carried.

"When was she diagnosed?"

"Two years ago."

"And how much time...?"

He didn't have to specify what he meant. Alzheimer's prognoses ran anywhere from four to eight years, some longer or shorter depending on other factors.

"They're giving her another year, max."

"I'm sorry," he said.

"I'm devastated about it," I replied. "There's so much she missed."

He nodded, wrapping his arms around my legs. "Do you get to see her a lot?"

"Not nearly enough. She's in a home in Wilmington."

"An hour away, at least," he said.

"On a good day."

He sighed. "There's only one thing we can do then."

I looked at him with a blank expression. "What do you mean?"

"There's only one way we can deal with this." He got to his feet, extending his hands to me.

I took them and he hoisted me up off the ground. Sand trickled down my legs and I didn't bother to brush the rest away.

He bent his head down in defeat, hands on his hips. "I was hoping it didn't have to come to this." Inching closer, he was able to rest his cheek against mine, his lips almost touching the height of my cheekbone. "I just don't think there's anything else we can do at this point," he whispered, holding his position and puffing soft flutters of air against my ear.

My heart raced. "What do you want to do?" I whispered back.

I heard the familiar beep of a stopwatch below us. "Tag, you're it," he hissed.

Smacking my ass, he turned and took off down the coastline.

"Oh no you—Jackson!"

My legs were pistons, zip lining me up the coast to be on his tail with a pace I didn't recognize. "Not this time!" I yelled at him. My arms swooshed in rhythm at my sides, an aching but elated heart pumping me faster and faster.

Jackson moved with the strides of a gazelle, meticulous and choreographed movements pushing him forward. "You can't beat me!" Jackson yelled over the waves. "You're not fast enough!"

I absorbed his taunts, closing the gap between us.

"You haven't trained hard enough!" he yelled. "You don't want it bad enough!"

I gritted my teeth as I paralleled his body, unleashing every muscle to advance me further.

"You want to win? THEN WIN!" he screamed.

Forging ahead, I kicked piles of sand at his thighs as I passed. Adrenaline coursed through every vein and I could hear Jackson trailing ten to fifteen feet behind me.

"You're only as fast as you want to be!" he yelled.

Runner's high hit me hard and I smiled with tears rolling down my cheeks at the same time. Winded and reaching my max, I stopped.

Too suddenly.

"Woah!" Jackson cried out. "Cant stop, can't—"

Jackson plowed into me just as I turned around. With reflexes like a cat, he wrapped one arm around me while bracing our fall with the other. When we hit the ground I was laughing so violently Jackson thought he had hurt me.

"You okay, Thomas the train?" he asked, realizing I was fine.

"Oh, don't ever do that again," I said, breathing deep into my gut to control my panting.

"Don't what?" he asked, looking at his stopwatch, one arm still around me. "Make you beat your record time in sprints?"

"No I didn't," I said, grabbing his wrist. I stared at the numbers, having shaved a whole thirty seconds off my fastest time. "That's amazing!"

"You're amazing," Jackson said, moving his thumb across my temple, looking at me with eyes that truly saw me.

I never understood what it was like to be seen, truly seen, before that moment. When someone can breathe life into you with their eyes, neither of you saying a word, and you can physically feel the hairs on the back of your neck stand up in response. His eyes saw my insecurities, my hurt, and my ambitions in a profound way because I never had to say them out loud.

He just knew.

"You're going to get tired of me winning these races all the time," I said, putting my hand on his cheek.

He shook his head. "Not a chance."

Barely having to move his face any closer, our lips eagerly touched. The sound of the waves faded, and the soft motion of Jackson's lips rolling over mine were all I could feel.

Chapter 7

"I want more of this," Jackson said.

Looking up from the book I was reading I tried to focus on the context of his statement. He had his back leaning against the bay window of his living room, feet crossed at the ankles. Running shorts hung at his hips, threatening to fall further with every slight movement of his torso.

"More what?" I asked

"This. More of you."

I wiggled my toes under a weighted, gray blanket draped across my lap. Sinking into the couch a little more I observed the scarce décor of Jackson's apartment. Our completed and routine morning run combined with the blazing propane fireplace in the center of the living room were all the makings for a lazy Sunday morning.

"Well I'd imagine having more of me *would* make running the Boston Marathon much easier," I replied, wrinkling my nose. "I could put one of me at the beginning of the race and one near the end and POOF, I'd win by a landslide."

Acknowledging my deflection he looked out the window, nodding. "I think we're past the point of thinking this isn't something more, aren't we?" He moved toward me, never breaking eye contact. "I can't be the only one wondering where this is going."

He knelt down in front of me, parting my knees with his hands as he inched closer, wrapping his hands around my waist. "That's not what I meant and you know that, Pip. We see each other five or six times a week, so what are we?"

"Well, you're my running buddy."

"You kiss all your running buddies?"

"Not the way I kiss you, if that makes you feel better," I joked.

"Do you make the train noise for everyone too?"

"Only when they're wearing ear buds so they can't hear me."

He lowered his head. "Why? Why can't you let me in? Where'd Thomas the train go?"

I turned my head away from him, studying a tiny dust ball on the floor near one leg of the couch across from me.

"Pip...?"

"This works," I said, the familiar racing of my heart contradicting my words.

"This is killing us," he said, inching toward my lips. "We run, yes, but something's here, you can't deny that."

"What?" I asked

He paused, musing over how to answer without sounding vulnerable. "I don't know, but I'd like to find out."

I felt like a con artist, staring back at his unguarded face as I tried for the millionth time to find the words to tell him how I really knew him, how I had seen him at his worst, and that I would understand if he never wanted to see me again. The words hung on the outer edge of my lips, dangling like a low hanging fruit. A exhale of air was all that escaped.

"Here, I have something for you," Jackson said, moving into the next room. I could hear the slide of a kitchen drawer, some rumbling, then he appeared carrying a box the size of a laptop with a bow attached to the top.

My heart dropped. "Jackson..." I said, eyeing the box with wide eyes.

He looked down at his hands, then back at me, all at once realizing that he was overextending or crossing some invisible boundary he couldn't see. "Oh! No...I mean, I'm not trying to be sappy here. I just wanted to do something nice. You've been working so hard and..."

His vulnerability is what kept me from telling him the truth. He was, at his core, a gentle but fragmented person. There were times I all but convinced myself to own up to how I knew him, but the moment I pulled into his driveway or saw his eyes light up when I approached him on the beach to run I just couldn't. I didn't want him to know I knew the *whole* Jackson until he was ready to tell me. There was a part of me that also knew I wouldn't let him in completely until he was able to have that discussion with me. If he couldn't trust me with the worst of himself, I couldn't give him the best of myself. We remained suspended in a continuum of expectations, swaying between salty kisses, morning runs, and protein pancakes.

He opened my clenched fist and put the box in the center of my lap, placing my hands on top as he pulled away. "You don't need to open it now, open it when you're ready."

"Okay," I agreed. "I need to head out, we on for a run tomorrow morning?"

"Already? I was hoping we could maybe spend the afternoon together and grab a bite to eat in town or something?"

I averted the notion. "Yeah, it's just that I'm on call all afternoon for work and I promised Meg I would meet up with her and Phoenix for lunch already."

"You two are always running off to play babysitter, so I take it you like kids?"

"Goodbye, Jackson," I said, playfully pushing his shoulder and giving myself room to stand. "We on for tomorrow morning?"

Jackson nodded, pulling me to my feet and planting a kiss on my forehead. "Wouldn't miss it."

His breath was heavy on my cheek as he pulled away and for a second I considered throwing the box onto the couch and staying a while longer.

"What do *you* think this is?" I asked.

He pulled my hips into him, cradling my backside in his hands and pushing his nose into mine. "Well, this is your ass."

"Thanks for the anatomy lesson."

My shirt lifted as he slid his hands up my side. "And this is your stomach."

"Noted," I said, dropping the box onto the couch to close the space between us.

"And these..." he said, pulling my face closer and grabbing my lower lip, rolling over it with his tongue. "I've been thinking about these all day."

I grabbed onto his elbows, pushing his hands harder into my sides. I walked him in a circle, positioning him toward the couch and pushing his forearms down so he would sit.

He crashed into the cushions as if his legs had disappeared. "Oh, crap, are you okay?" I asked. "I didn't think I pushed down that hard."

"You didn't," he said, the tone in his voice changing. "It happens sometimes."

"What happens?"

"Beautiful women who try and seduce me make my legs give out."

"Oh, so you *do* have a kryptonite?" I said, teasing. I straddled him, wrapping my arms around his neck and placing kisses from his collarbone to his ear. He stiffened a little and I pushed away from him. "You okay?"

"Yeah, just don't want to make you late. Maybe you should go then."

"I can spare a few minutes."

"Okay, so why don't you open the box?"

My cheeks flared. I nodded, studying his demeanor. "You sure you're okay?"

"Yeah," he replied, a clear shift in his voice. "I just think you should open it."

I didn't mean to pout when I slid from his lap to the couch, but the awkward silence that fell between us was weighty enough to tell me he wasn't in the mood. He barely glanced in my direction as I ripped open the side of the box, the cardboard crumbling apart. "Jackson, this is perfect!"

"Is it? It's nothing, really."

I meddled through the box, sorting through the Gu packs, Slim Jims, and high performance socks that were delicately wrapped in tissue paper. "You didn't have to do this."

"I know," he said, finally resting his gaze on my face. "I wanted to. You'll need them for the race."

"I do *love* Slim Jims. Now I don't want to leave, this was really sweet," I confessed, staring at the time on my phone, knowing I had somewhere to be before going to visit my mom late that afternoon.

"But you have to?"

I hesitated, fighting with the voices in my head. "I have to."

"If you must. Maybe we can meet at your place tomorrow? Change it up a bit?"

I wrinkled my nose. "Well that doesn't make much sense, you're closer to the beach. Plus my house stinks like bodily fluids and dirty scrubs, not attractive."

"So I guess it's my place then? Same time, same place?"

"You promise to slap my ass every time you outrun me again?"

"If you'll have me."

"I'll have you," I said, raising my lips to his.

* * *

I took my time heading to the nursing home, letting people pass me who were headed to more time constrictive destinations. The smell of tulips from the flower shop on the passenger seat next to me reminded me of nostalgic mornings making banana pancakes with my mom when I was too young to remember most of anything else.

An extra deep, white mixing bowl would be propped between my legs as I sat perked on the counter next to the griddle with Mom handing me eggs to crack. Only half of them made it into the bowl, so she wiped away the excess that was dripping down my legs and handed me another. She told me that life was like an egg, delicate and messy all at the same time.

I didn't get the reference at the time.

"Boy, do I get it now," I whispered, finally maneuvering into the parking lot.

"Knock-knock. Hey you!" I said, poking my head around her door and waving the tulips. "How are you?"

"Oh!" she said, somewhat startled. Standing at the foot of her bed she looked from the down comforter to her window, then back to me. "Am I okay?" she asked, looking down at her plaid shirt, pulling it out to check the fabric.

"You're okay," I assured her, making my way to place them on her nightstand.

"Tulips," she said, recognizing the flower.

I paused with my hands wrapped around the stems, not wanting to turn around and face her. "Yes, tulips," I responded with my back to her. "Do you know why I brought you tulips today?"

The silence was deafening but I didn't want to break the moment, so I hovered in position waiting to hear her response.

"It's Sunday."

I turned around, my face flushing as my heartbeat skyrocketed. "Yes, it's Sunday, why do you get tulips on Sundays?"

My question was met with pressed lips and a heightened left eyebrow. "My daughter brings me tulips every Sunday," she said matter-of-factly.

"Who am I?" I blurted out.

She stared, studying my face and nodding as she came to her decision. "You're lovely."

I pressed harder. "Why would your daughter bring you tulips on Sundays?"

"Well, I taught her to do that. Ever since she went away to college, I told her to bring me tulips on Sundays. It was the one thing I ever asked of her."

"That's right," I said.

"I wanted it to become routine."

I paused. "What do you mean?"

"It had to become routine, her bringing me flowers. How else would I get her to visit me?"

"I don't think much could keep her from you," I said, my heart aching. Throughout college and afterwards, my mom would insist I brought her flowers every Sunday. It was a non-negotiable. She promised to pay my tuition if, in return, every Sunday I would show up to her house—no matter where I was—to bring her flowers. It was a small sacrifice to make; I got a nursing degree and weekly memories with my mom.

"When I'm gone," she said softly. "How else will I get her to visit my grave once a week when I'm gone if I didn't make it part of her routine? I love her so, I wanted to make sure she came to see me even when I'm not here to tell her to do it."

My eyes welled up. "Do you know who I am?"

She narrowed her eyes, lowering herself to her bed as she considered the question.

"No tricks today, Pippa. I'm waiting for Roger to get home and I have dinner to make before we go play poker at the firehouse. Did you call Mom today? She was complaining you never call her anymore."

I nodded, lowering myself to a wooden rocking chair nearby to clutch my chest. "Okay, no tricks today," I promised, choking back tears. "I just wanted you to remember one more time. I needed to know you could remember me."

I knew at this point I was talking to a wall. Her lucid moments were sporadic and fleeting depending on the weather and her mood. A heap of emotions consumed me and I swallowed hard, looking out the window to center myself.

"You're crying," Mom said.

"I am."

"Does your heart hurt?" she asked.

"It does. So much."

"Tell me about it," she said, patting the bed beside her.

I nodded, making my way to her bedside. When I sat down she took my hand into hers, rubbing the top of my knuckles. They were warm and inviting, like sliding my hands into a pair of gloves that had been worn for years.

"It's all right to feel sad, we all do sometimes," she said.

"I have no one," I admitted. "I've been so busy keeping people out so that they wouldn't disappoint me that now that I need someone I feel like everyone but no one is there at the same time."

She nodded, so I continued.

"Dylan and I broke up a while back. Then we got back together, only to break up again a year ago. He wants to be there for Boston but I told him it wasn't a good idea, I don't particularly want him there because we're always a mess. Then there's Jackson, just waving in the wind waiting for me to let my guard down, so I feel like I'm losing him too. Meg is busy with her own life and she pretends to not be falling apart for Phoenix's sake and I'm swamped with work too. I just feel like I'm losing a grasp on it all, even you."

Mom wiped the tears trickling down my right cheek. "You can't lose something that won't let go. I'll sit here with you." She squeezed my hand.

"I haven't seen you in so long, I miss you," I confessed. I was referring to the long conversations we would have in her kitchen or on the phone when I was crying in my dorm room over the stress of graduating.

"Hmmm," she said, agreeing. "I'm here, even if it's just to remind you of who you are from time to time."

"Who am I?" I asked

She smiled. "I know who you are, my heart says so."

* * *

I was a hypocrite driving home, squinting at blurred signs and cars through a windshield of tears. Even though I had told Meg countless times to pull over when she was upset over whatever current breakup or life mishap that was spiraling out of control, I didn't realize how cathartic it could be to physically transport yourself away from the thing that was hurting your heart the most.

The box from Jackson skidded across my kitchen counter, car keys following, as I beelined for the bathroom to take a scalding shower.

The only thing that flowed harder than tears from love lost was a shower, it was designed to hide heartache.

Sitting on the floor of the shower I traced beads of water with my eyes, my back against the wall and knees clutched to my chest. Each droplet articulately navigated down, collecting in size as it passed others nearby until it was so swollen it crazily ping-ponged down the length of the surface to the shower floor. I watched them for what seemed like hours, slowing my breath and contributing sporadic droplets from my face to the parade of water flowing down the drain.

It washed away, all of it. So I took a breath and nodded as I grabbed a towel and wrapped my shoulders, satisfied that the heaviness of the afternoon was gone.

Chapter 8

I pushed the mute button on my phone for the hundredth time. I was on the phone with Dylan and he was insisting on showing up to support me at the Boston Marathon. I was having a hard time finding the words to tell him I didn't want him to be there without sounding like a complete jerk.

"It's not a good idea," I repeated. "Plus, I know you're busy that weekend, you already told me that. You have other things to worry about."

"I'm not busy, Pip, I can make the time if I want to. Why are you pushing back so hard on this? Any other time I would have told you I wanted to be there you'd have jumped at the chance, now you suddenly don't care?"

"It's not that I don't care," I said. "I just want to be able to focus on the race and it'll be harder to do that with you there."

"I mess up your thinking like that?" he teased into the phone.

Dylan and I were like fire and gasoline. We had dated for so long during and after college that we fought more like brother and sister than we did ex-lovers. We had a hairy and twisted past, making decisions about our relationship based on obligation and impulse. He pushed

66

and I pulled, I jumped and he sank. We were on a rollercoaster that led us through opposite universes from the start but every once in a while our tracks would overlap and we'd come crashing into each other like the world was ours for the taking. It was toxic but beautiful; we needed each other but thrived when we were apart at the same time.

"You know what I mean, Dylan."

"Say you want me there."

"I don't."

"This doesn't have anything to do with your running buddy, does it?" he asked, lowering his tone to a judgmental level.

"What does that have to do with anything?" I asked, getting defensive. "I'm allowed to say I don't want you there, Dylan."

"Just say you do anyway. I won't go if you really don't want me to but at least say you do so I can sleep tonight with a smile on my face."

I sighed, my phone suddenly vibrating. I pulled it away from my ear long enough to see it was a text from my co-worker Lisa. I minimized the call, keeping Dylan in suspense as I checked the message:

Thought you should know. Jackson was just admitted again.
It's bad. Get here as soon as you can.

My heart dropped. "Dylan I need to go."

"Why can't you just answer me?"

"It's a work emergency, need to go. Sorry." I hung up and grabbed my car keys off of the counter, frantically searching for my sneakers.

● ● ●

"What's wrong?" I said, breathless from running up four flights of stairs. "What happened?"

"It's bad," Lisa said, shaking her head as I approached her.

"I'll say it's bad," Moe chimed in, rounding the corner. "Who dressed you today Pip, or is wearing two different shoes the thing to do nowadays?"

I glanced at my feet, dismissing the two different shoes I had thrown on in my rush to leave the house. "Seriously Lisa, what happened?"

"You know I can't tell you," she said, biting her lip. "You're not on his contact list and you're not family. It was risky to even tell you he was admitted in the first place but I didn't know what to do. He was calling out for you in his sleep, thank goodness boss lady wasn't in the room, there's not many Pippas floating around this city so I'm sure she would have put two and two together, especially after looking at his past charts and who had signed some of them."

"Two and two makes four," Moe said, grinning.

"Shut up, Moe." I said, directing my anger at him.

His smile faded and I put my hand up in frustration. "I'm sorry. It's not you, it's..."

"No I get it, it's okay," he replied. "Let me know if you need anything, I need to do my rounds." Moe grabbed a nearby clipboard, maneuvering his way around a crash cart.

"What do you mean when he wakes up again? Did they have to put him under? What is he on?"

"I can't..."

"Lisa I know you can't but it's me, not just any other co-worker. That's why you know about Jackson in the first place and I know it's why you called me."

She nodded, looking uneasy as she glanced down the hall.

"Okay let's role play," I said. "Pretend you're looking for advice on your next course of action and need to roll things off of me to decide. Co-worker to co-worker."

She bit her bottom lip and looked down the hallway once more to make sure no one else was in earshot. "Promise not to out me?"

"Never in a million years," I said, making an X over my heart.

"He came in displaying signs of severe psychosis, really irritable and upset. They couldn't even get his last name before be became hostile with an attending and we had to sedate him."

"How long ago?"

Lisa sighed and looked away.

"Tell me!"

"Okay! Last night."

"Last night?! He was admitted last night and you just *NOW*..." I trailed off, trying to keep my voice lowered to prevent people from looking in our direction. "Never mind. Did he wake up? What did he say?"

"For a little while yes, but he was displaying severe hyperarousal symptoms so we had to put him back under, for his safety and ours."

My phone vibrated in my pocket before I could ask any more questions.

"I have to run," Lisa said, grabbing a chart nearby. "Promise me you won't go in there, Pip. I can't lose my job, I just wanted you to know he was here and he was safe. He'll only be here another twenty-four hours at most, so I'll stay on it and make sure no other nurses who know you well have a chance to get near him."

"Okay, okay," I said, drumming my fingertips together in front of me while I compiled a list in my head. "Make his room as dark as you can, he doesn't respond well to light when he's having an episode. Turn the air up, even though it'll feel too cold for you there's something about the temperature change that helps bring him down. Oh, and don't let them put rice on his tray for *any* meals, got it? The last time he was hospitalized he had tried wrapping a cord around his neck after they served him rice that night." I swallowed, grateful that I had walked into his room that day before it escalated. He barely had time to react when I issued a distress call and went against all hospital policies by attempting to contain him on my own. I was able to remove the cord from his neck and wrap my arms tightly around his torso. Had he not been medicated I would have sustained devastating injuries, I was sure of it. He could have swung me around like a ragdoll. Instead he let me hold onto him, rocking him back and forth, whispering in his ear, 'Do the hard thing. Do the hard thing and stay with me, Jackson.'

"He *can't* find out I work at this hospital and I was *never* here," I said sternly, gazing down the hallway, grateful that I didn't know his room number so I didn't run to him. "Especially if he's already set off, I don't want him getting worse." I fumbled for my phone, scanning the screen. "Luckily today and tomorrow are my days off anyway, so I'll stay far away, I promise."

She nodded, pressing her lips together in agreement. "I'll let you know if anything changes...co-worker to co-worker. Got to run Pip, hang in there."

I nodded, exhaling as I answered the phone that had started vibrating in my hand and watching Lisa walk in the opposite direction. I was on autopilot, not bothering to look at who was calling. "Yeah?" I said.

"Hi friend, why the robotic tone? You miss me that much that your life is falling apart without me? I knew it. Wanna drink wine tonight?"

"Meg," I said, not knowing what else to say. She recognized the tone in my voice almost immediately.

"What's wrong? Are you hurt?"

"I'm at the hospital."

"Did you get hit by a car when you were running? I can be there in two minutes, I'm on my way."

"No, Meg. It's Jackson."

"Jackson got hit by a car? Whoa, did he jump in front of a car for you? Did he sacrifice himself? Damn, I need a man like that."

While it was a much needed break in the ice, I didn't have time to explain. "I'll call you in a bit, okay? I'm fine. I'll call you, promise."

I hung up and glanced down the hallway to see if Lisa or Moe were in sight. They weren't, so I sauntered over to the nurse's station to see if I could find out any more information.

Becca was working behind the desk, hastily typing and pushing her glasses back onto the bridge of her nose every five seconds.

"Hey Bec," I said, vying for small talk. "Busy?"

"Mmmmm," she said, not looking up.

"Heard it's crazy here today, someone came in extra hostile, what happened?"

"Yeahhhh," she said slowly, typing away. "Yep, he came in here last night and..." she trailed off when she looked up at me. "Hey where are your scrubs? Are you picking up an extra shift or something?"

I blinked. "Not really, just... you know, just waiting for Lisa to get a break so we can go grab a bite."

Becca nodded and turned back to her monitor. "Yeah, good luck with that, we've been swamped all day. Ask her about how crazy last night was when you see her, it was her patient anyway."

The conversation was dead in the water before it started to I tapped the desk with my finger and pretended to check my phone. "Yeah, so I heard. I wonder where they put him," I questioned out loud. "Hopefully not on any of the new nurses routes, not sure they could handle it."

"One-thirty-five," she said without looking up. "He's a wild one, a *Desperate* for sure," she said, referring to our unconventional way of categorizing patients as they were admitted.

"He is *not*," I said, too quickly.

Becca looked up, narrowing her eyes. "Wait, how do you—"

"I mean, he doesn't sound like a *Desperate* from what everyone has been saying. Maybe a *Sad*, who knows. I'm sure Lisa knows best since he's her patient."

Becca nodded, her eyes transfixed on mine.

"Anyway, I'm going to go see if I can track down Lisa. See ya around." I didn't wait for her to respond. Instead I turned to duck down the adjacent hallway, so quickly that I almost butted heads with Meg as she rounded the corner.

"Whoa! Watch where you're— Oh! Pip! Are you okay? What happened?"

"What are you...wait, how did you get here so fast? Did you teleport here?"

"You answer the phone with dead-voice and say you're in the hospital with Jackson and expect me not to show up? What kind of friend am I?"

"The unpredictable kind," I said, moving her to a quiet end of the hallway. "The best kind, really. But I'm not really here *with* Jackson."

"Mmmm hmmm okay. Well, we can discuss your commitment issues later, what room is he in?"

"One-thirty-five" I repeated, without thinking. "Oh no, but Meg we can't—"

"Let's go see Mr. Invincible then," she said, starting down the hallway, taking my hand in her grip.

"No, Meg, you don't understand. I can't go in there."

"Yes you can. Put your big girl pants on and go hold his hand. He jumped in front of a car for you for goodness sake. Do you need him to hold a sign above his head that says he loves you for you to stop being so thick or will a postcard suffice?"

"He didn't get hit by a car and wait—" I spun Meg around. "He said he loves me? When?"

Meg brought her eyebrows together and opened her mouth so the tip of her tongue was ever so slightly visible. "I'm looking at you like this because you're either ignorant or truly that dense. Sad, really," she said, reaching out to tuck a strand of hair behind my ear. "I always thought you to be the smarter of us two. I'm okay with being the smart one, in case you're wondering. Jackson doesn't have to *say* anything, Pippa. I haven't seen you much since you both started training but I get it, it's *new* and more fun than spending the day at the library with me and Phoenix. So, let's go."

"I really can't go in there. Let's go grab some lunch and we can talk about it."

"Nothing to talk about, you can go in there Pip. You just push the door open and say—"

"Hi, I'm Pippa, I wasn't supposed to be in your room but you accidentally became my patient when I had to check in on you for a co-worker and—you don't remember this— but I watched you fall apart for days before your discharge and you were so hopped up on drugs and emotions that you don't even remember meeting me?" I gushed.

Meg's mouth gaped to dangerous levels. She rarely didn't know what to say, and I braced myself for impact. "No..." she said slowly, her eyes blank. "You most definitely don't want to tell him that."

I shifted my weight, aware of the tension that surrounded us in that moment.

She continued. "You mean to tell me that Jackson is patient two-thirty-three from a few weeks ago, but that your boss still thinks it's an issue for you to see him? How does that violate any ethics? He just walked into your life one day out on the beach and—" the sudden gasp from her throat let me know she finally put the dots together. "Pippa! You told me he met you out on the beach that day and that it was random but *he doesn't know, does he*? How have you not told him yet? Are you hiding it from him? Does he think you guys met on the beach that day for the first time? How can he really not remember you being in his room at the hospital?"

She was speaking a mile a minute. Trembling, I nodded my head to confirm her accusations.

Meg's eyes darkened. "I can't believe you would do that to him," she whispered. "I can't believe you'd witness the most vulnerable part of him and go on pretending like it doesn't exist...for your own agenda."

"I didn't have an agenda!" I shot back.

"You never do, you medical people. There's never any room for anything but your own opinions."

"Meg!"

She turned her body away from me, crossing her arms in front of her chest. "Jackson deserves better than that, just like my sister did. Cheryl told her doctors that it felt like she was walking over broken glass just to keep breathing everyday and they did *nothing*."

"Meg," I said, my heart thudding against my chest. "I'm so sorry they didn't treat Cheryl the way they should have when she came home. We've made so much progress since then, you know that's why I changed specialties after she died."

"Good for you for switching to the mental health unit here, but Cheryl didn't *die*, they *killed* her," Meg said, heading toward the elevators.

I trailed her, trying to keep up with her stride.

"I should have known that's why you were keeping him at an arm's length, why you were so closed off to him and starting to shut me out," she said. "You two spent a few weeks in your own little world, locking everyone out so you could keep your secret. Don't you feel guilty about canceling plans with me and—"

"Meg, don't, it's complicated."

"It's really very simple," she said, pinching her pointer and middle fingers against her thumb to drive home her point. He was your patient-turned-love-interest and your own pride couldn't let you push past that to tell him the truth."

"That's not fair. I couldn't, my job—"

"What you're doing is not fair. He deserves to know. Are you running together for training or therapy sessions? Don't you think *he* should choose whether or not to keep this thing going? It's not okay, and you need to tell him." She walked into the elevator, pushing the lobby button. "Tell him, or next time I see him, I will."

The doors started to close and I slid an elbow between them to prop them open. "You're right, Meg." I nodded through the tears sitting in the corners of my eyes. "I've been too scared to tell him because I don't want to lose him. I can't."

"You can't lose what was never yours," Meg said.

I let the words sink in, lowering my head to my feet. I had been so focused on what I thought Jackson needed from me, it never crossed my mind that maybe he would have wanted a voice in the matter.

"I'll tell him after the race, it's only a few days away and he's so excited for it. I promise, you don't want to take that away from him."

Meg sighed, but nodded. "He's been working hard training you."

"Will you still be there?" I asked.

Looking up at the ceiling, she pivoted her right foot into the floor in frustration, putting out a pretend cigarette. "At the Boston?"

"Yeah, will you still be there?"

"Of course I will," Meg said, annoyed at the question. "That's what you do for the people you love. You show up, even when it's hard. Even when you don't think they deserve you."

Chapter 9

Boston Marathon
April 15th, 2013

The 117th Boston Marathon started out like any other. Originally inspired by the success of the first marathon competition in the 1896 Olympics, waves of runners lined up on Patriot's Day to push the limits of their legs and their hearts to cross the finish line on Boylston Street.

I was no exception.

Wave three runners sprawled the streets, stretching and psyching each other up before the 10:40 a.m. start time. There were just about nine thousand entrants, moving around in a sea of spandex and blue bibs that we were given out as our wave color.

The weather was storybook perfect, hovering in the low 50's at its peak and not a rain cloud in sight. I had trained in rain, cold, and sand to help me fuel through the elements.

Jackson and I drove up a day earlier, crashing at a hotel just outside of Hopkinton, Massachusetts. I had insisted on separate hotel rooms, not wanting to risk anything that might distract me from the race.

"It's only twenty-six miles, Pip," Jackson said, shoveling a mouth full of granola in his mouth race morning.

"Wrong," I answered. "It's twenty-six point two miles exactly."

"Well, you're *exactly* ready then."

"I don't feel ready, I feel like something is off."

"Morning-of jitters, I'll be right near Copley square to watch you cross the finish line. Can't wait for you to win this thing."

I puffed through my teeth. "I'd be happy to cross the finish line at all, we don't need to get all fancy and throw around words like *winner* or anything."

"When you cross the finish line, no matter how many people will be before or after you, it will make you a winner. Don't undermine that. You're ready."

I was ready because the sneakers I trained in for months prior were the perfect level of broken-in. They hugged my feet like armor. Jackson helped me carb-load the night before at dinner, indulging in fatty proteins and pasta. I had two Gu packs ready to fuel me every ten miles or so during the race if I needed them. I had studied the route countless times, over and over again until I could almost see myself crossing the finish line in my mind by what streets to take.

I was ready.

In retrospect, I don't think anyone was ready for the Boston City Marathon that year.

Almost two hours into my run, after adrenaline had freshly steamed off after the initial start of my wave, I knew that I was nowhere close to being the winner of the Boston. My legs were turbines, though, churning me through mile after mile. Grateful for the intensive training sessions I originally cursed Jackson for, I refused to acknowledge the slight sputtering of my legs every few hundred feet after the first hour passed.

My face must have shown my frustration, because off to the left I heard a very familiar voice shouting my name over the chorus of other supporters.

"Pip! Pippa! TAKE YOUR GU PACK! PIP!"

I scanned the crowd, careful not to ambush the runners streaming ahead of me.

"DAMN IT PIP, TAKE YOUR GU PACK!"

Searching one last time, I finally saw Dylan's face among the bystanders.

"I KNOW YOU!" he screamed. "DON'T HOLD OUT! TAKE IT!"

Frantically, I searched for my holster. Too defeated to care that he had directly ignored me by showing up, I ripped open the top of a Gu pack and squeezed the entire contents into my mouth.

"ATTA GIRL! GO PIP! I'LL SEE YOU AT THE FINISH!"

Meg was at his side, screaming my name over and over.

His words dissipated behind me. The familiar warmth of his voice and presence was a boost I didn't think I needed. The combination of his words, the Gu pack, and water I squeezed into my mouth fully charged me for a second wind.

Tracing the route in my head, thoughts of doubt started to creep in when a dull cramp plagued my right side. I slowed my stride like Jackson taught me, sucking in deep breaths of air through my nose and pushing them out of my mouth and through my gut. Jackson had made me drink pickle juice that morning to help combat any cramps, but it wasn't foolproof.

I pictured the finish line.

At one point I tripped over my own clumsy gait, grabbing at a runner in front of me out of instinct. A balding man to my right grabbed my right wrist just as I thought I was going to go down for good, giving me just enough guidance to steady myself and keep pace.

"Woah, darling, you're almost there. Come on now, you're almost there don't give out just yet."

I crossed the intersection of Exeter and Boylston Streets, eyeing the finish line, my legs no longer transmitting any feeling to my brain. My second Gu pack was still in my holster, screaming at me to take it.

That's when I heard it.

It was low at first, but it was distinct enough for me to hear over the roar of the bystanders losing their minds as their loved ones crossed the finish line up ahead.

Jackson's voice rose above the rest, and I spotted him. Holding his fist in the air, he was victoriously yelling out, making noise like the horn of a train.

Shaking my head, I was sure my cheeks were almost touching the bottom of my eyes from smiling so hard. Sucking in a deep breath, I stretched my arm into the sky and echoed his war cry, meeting his gaze for a brief moment.

It wasn't a bone-rattling explosion like you might imagine— more of a muffled thud with a large plume of smoke that ran straight up the mid-level buildings surrounding us.

The pressure cooker bomb detonated at 2:49 p.m., only several hundred feet ahead of me.

Shrieking ensued almost immediately from an indistinct location, although between the high pitched whining consuming my ears I could only assume the wrangled and distraught faces of the people around me were emitting such a noise.

Jackson was the only person I could spot in the crowd as I fell to the pavement, my hands covering my ears in immense pain. His silhouette was frozen in place among a sea of people flailing all around him, a hollow look in his eyes not permitting him to come to me.

Dylan reached me first, just as I lost consciousness for the first time. I could see his lips start to move as he placed a hand behind my head to lift my bleeding head from the pavement. Struggling to keep my eyes open, I rapidly blinked to keep myself awake.

The chaos surrounding us couldn't hold a flame to the look in Jackson's eyes when he walked up behind Dylan. Watching him scream to the people all around us, I noticed Jackson's face was speckled in blood, but I didn't see any gashes.

It's someone else's.

Dylan stood up and ran out of my view, turning to Jackson before he did so, and mouthing something to him, then pointing in my direction.

Jackson kneeled down at my side, his hands feeling moist from the blood pooling out of my ear and underneath my hair as he cradled me. I closed my eyes.

When I opened them, Dylan was standing behind Jackson, his face dirty from tears that he couldn't hold back. Jackson had two overlapping palms placed firmly on my chest, elbows locked and frozen in place, when he realized my eyes were open. He said something, but no sounds emerged. I could only see his lips spitting rapid fire. When I didn't respond Dylan started shouting at Jackson from behind, pointing at me and running his hands through his hair.

It was then that I saw the switch.

Pupils dilated, the smooth curvature of Jackson's jaw shifted upright. His eyes hollowed, a dark fog filling them. He looked off into the distance, and I saw his chest begin to heave in a quickened rhythm.

Dylan, run.

Hunched over with his hands on his knees, Dylan let out a long breath of air in relief.

I was alive.

Then, he reached out to pat Jackson on the back.

He never saw it coming.

The first blow to Dylan's face was imminent and swift. They fell to my right, and it took all of my strength to turn my head to the side to watch them.

Boulders of muscle flexed up and down as Jackson continued to deliver blows to Dylan's face. His legs were limp beneath Jackson as he crouched above him, a slow motion assault forcing Dylan's legs to jump in movement with every connection.

Stop, Jackson, you'll kill him.

Not able to watch, I turned my head to focus on the clouds above me. I couldn't move to help him, and a wave of exhaustion fell over me, my eyes beginning to flutter.

There were approximately five thousand seven hundred runners who would never cross the finish line of the Boston Marathon that day.

I was one of them.

Chapter 10

There were two explosions—a little over two hundreds yards apart— just shy of the finish line. An unprecedented manhunt for the bombers ensued only three days after, shutting down the city of Watertown. That's when police moved in on the one bomber who had been spotted hiding in a boat in someone's backyard. Three people had died instantly from the blast that day. Several hundred others were injured, including sixteen people who lost limbs.

Then there was me.

The first time I opened my eyes after the bombing was almost four days later. Jackson was hunched over the bed, holding my left hand. A stream of IVs littered my hands and I could only make out shadows of the people and things around me.

"When is she going to wake up?" I heard Jackson say. It was muffled, but the words filtered through.

"Hard to say," another voice followed. "We're doing everything we can to slowly wean her off sedation to keep the swelling in her brain down. We don't want to take any chances. This is the best course of treatment, I can assure you."

"The two surgeries she had, do we know if her hearing will be restored?"

"We won't know until she wakes up, but I'm hopeful the myringoplasty was successful. The piece of shrapnel she had lodged in the side of her head was mostly superficial and the swelling of her brain seems to have corrected itself after the ventriculostomy. The drain worked well and we can remove the bandages from her head in a day or so. The ear was concerning since her eardrum was blown out, either from the blast itself or another piece of shrapnel it's hard to say. It's a miracle you walked away with only a few scratches. I'm glad they figured out who the bombers were. I've never seen a manhunt organize like that."

I moaned, a dull ache radiating hard between my pupils every time I tried to keep my eyes open for longer than two seconds.

"She's waking up," I heard Jackson's voice say. "Pip? Pippa can you hear me?"

Moaning in response, I heard the shuffling of feet and the beeping of a few machines. "We can raise her morphine drip a bit. There ya go sweetie, try and rest. I know the pain is probably intense. Pippa, can you move your hands and toes for me?"

"Pip, I'm so glad you're awake. I needed to tell you—"

Darkness fell over me and I don't know how much time passed before I opened my eyes again. Meg's voice lulled me from my sleep, soft and concerned but full of fire.

"You could have killed him, do you have any idea how lucky you are Dylan doesn't remember a damn thing?" she hissed.

"How many times can I say I'm sorry? I can't explain what happened, I don't even remember doing it. I really don't, Meg."

"Pippa would *never* forgive you if he had died. Never. You have no idea what history these two have. They have—"

"Where are they sending him next?" Jackson asked, cutting her off.

"They did what they could in the emergency room but the best reconstructive surgeon he could find is taking him in, don't worry about where. His nose can be rebuilt, they'll have to get creative but they can do it. It'll be a few weeks before he can have his next surgery."

Silence filled the room.

"I was late getting to the shuttle," Meg said mournfully. "Dylan and I thought it would be fun to see her at the beginning of the race and then meet her at the end. Once she passed us we tried to get to the finish line in time, but I had to pee and didn't want Dylan to be late. He mentioned something about wanting to ask Pippa to try again..." Her voice trailed off, her voice cracking. "I was getting off the shuttle when I heard the blast."

I opened my mouth, eyes closed, trying my hardest to speak.

"Feeee...."

It fell silent and I realized they knew I was awake.

"Go get the doctor, quick," Meg instructed.

I heard a door open and quick footsteps running down a hallway.

"Pip? Can you hear me lady? Can you open your eyes?"

They fluttered trying to open, only catching the shadows of the room. I was able to determine it was evening, but otherwise couldn't focus on one thing over another.

"That's okay, you can rest your eyes," Meg said.

"Feee..."

"Feee? What's Feee?" Jackson asked, his voice reappearing. "Do you need something? What is it?"

A door opened and I heard a voice following behind Jackson's. "Last time she was awake was a day ago, is that bad? Can she hear us you think? Do you think—"

"Slow down, slow down. Let's see what we have here."

An intrusive light was forced into my eye, a cold hand erecting my eyelid upward. I moaned, turning my head to the side in protest.

"It's hurting her," Meg said.

"It's likely just a sensitivity to the light, but I want to make sure her eyes are dilating like they should."

"She should be getting better by now," Jackson complained. "She's been here long enough and the sedation has been weaned to the smallest amounts."

"She's healing," a calm voice said. "Everyone does it at their own pace. I know it seems like a lifetime because you're scared but it has only been a few days. She needs to rest."

"Feeeeee..." I said again.

"What's that darling? Does something *feel* bad?"

"Your feet? Do your feet hurt?" Jackson guessed.

"That's not what she's saying," I heard Meg say.

"Fehhh," I said louder, hoping Meg would understand.

A familiar hand slid into mine, the outline of rings that Meg was known to wear caressing my fingers. "It's okay, don't you worry. Everyone is fine and we just need you to get better," she said, addressing my worries. "Dylan is okay too, he has some surgeries to get through in the future but he'll be just fine."

"What was she saying?" Jackson asked.

"Don't worry about it," Meg said sternly. "If she had wanted you to know, she would have told you. It's not my place."

"Does she need something?" a voice said, presumably the doctor.

"Nothing you can give her," Meg said sadly.

I swayed in and out of consciousnesses and slept a full day more before I was strong enough to hold my eyes open. Nurses and doctors rotated through my room taking vitals, adjusting medications and sending me down for scans. The reality of my injuries was only recognized when one nurse showed me a scan of my brain from when they had first admitted me compared to one I had done earlier that morning.

They had been forced to drill a hole in my skull to relieve some of the pressure. They were unsure if I had lost any motor functions, if I was able to speak, or if I remembered what happened that day.

Unfortunately, I remembered everything.

I especially remember the first full conversation I had with Jackson after I was awake and sitting up in bed.

"You could have killed him," I whispered, watching him stare out of the hospital window to the people below. Most of my morning had been spent doing the same thing, before visiting hours. The view of the suburbs alive and busy in the world outside of the hospital was a comforting one. Pedestrians were pacing down the sidewalks with umbrellas above their heads. It looked like a calm ocean wave, colorfully outlining the street.

"I know," he said not turning around. "I can't tell you how sorry—"

"I'm not the one you need to be apologizing to."

He turned to face me and as much as I didn't want my heart to flutter at the pained look on his face, there it was, pounding against my chest. One part of me wanted to scream in his face and push his broad shoulders out the door and out of my life forever. The memory of Jackson's rage was haunting. The other part of me wanted to comfort him and appreciate how triggering it must have been to be in that scenario.

"I know that, Pip. If it makes you feel any better, I really don't think he remembers a thing. He wouldn't even know what I was apologizing for."

"How would that make me feel better?" I said, my voice heightening. "So what, he can't remember it happening so you're going to pretend like it didn't?"

The majority of my anger was on myself at that point. I was culpable of the same double standard. Jackson was up on a Ferris wheel, and I was expecting him to jump off when it peaked at the top when I couldn't even manage the strength to look down.

"You're right," he said, making my guilt worse.

I nodded. "How long have you been here?" I asked.

"I haven't left."

His loyalty made me swallow hard. Running over the remaining gauze on my head and ears, his eyes were stones. They honed in on the machines beeping around me, a ghosted look on his face. "How could I possibly leave you? I did this."

"You did what?"

"Trained you, helped you be a better runner. I helped you get to that finish line," he said, his eyes brimming with fire. "If we never would have met...if we didn't train so hard to make you faster maybe you wouldn't have been so close to the blast."

"I did it to myself," I said, puffing out my chest. "With or without you I would have made it to that finish line. I wanted the Boston," I replied.

"Not as much as I wanted you to be safe."

The sentiment warmed my chest. "You don't need to stay, Jackson."

He shrugged, taking in a deep breath, forcing the white thermal he was wearing to hug his chest like I wished I could. "I know I don't need to be here, Pip. I want to be."

Just then a nurse walked in with a chart in her hand. She smiled when she saw I was awake, making her way over to my bed. Acknowledging Jackson, the smile faded from her face by the time she reached my bedside. In a stiffened motion she turned from me to him, not saying a word. The way her eyes danced around in her head told me she didn't know how to deflect from the awkwardness of the situation.

"Are you okay?" she asked, tipping her head to the side to point out Jackson while staring blankly ahead at me. "Did you need...anything?"

She thought he was a threat.

Cross-armed and tapping his foot while he stared out the window, Jackson *did* look intimidating. He was chiseled, presenting himself like a brick wall among a field of flowers. Nothing on his face at the moment said he was friendly or even open to communication, so I could tell his presence confused her. I wondered if she thought he had somehow swindled his way into my room uninvited.

"We're fine," I assured her. "This is Jackson."

"Thank you for taking such good care of her," Jackson said at the mention of his name, stepping forward with an outstretched hand and taking the nurse by surprise.

She stared at it, nodding instead of taking it. "Yes, well, I know this has been hard for..." Her voice trailed off, the silence amplifying the curiosity of whether or not Jackson was supposed to be there. It was clear she didn't understand his presence and the tension in the room heightened tenfold.

"I have other patients to check in on. If you need anything just buzz." She turned on her heel—a polite smile drawn on her face—and didn't look back as she scurried out the door.

"Must be a busy day or something," Jackson said, watching her exit. "Hey, you're a nurse. Was she acting funny or was it just me?"

"You should probably go. Go get some rest," I suggested as my phone buzzed. I glanced over a text from Meg saying that she just got to the hospital for a visit.

Jackson nodded without looking at me. He shifted his weight from one foot to another, glancing back at the window behind him for only a moment. Stopping at the end of my bed, he hesitated just long enough to let me consider whether or not he was going to try and kiss me goodbye. He decided against it and instead made it to the door, pausing in the doorway as he turned to face me.

"I'm not the only one relieved you're okay, you know that?"

I froze. "What do you mean?"

"In your sleep, you said Phoenix's name a few times. You said a bunch of things but you mentioned her more than once, I know you and Meg spend a lot of time with her. Meg has been a mess, she puts on a good show but she was terrified. I know you're not used to being waited on, I just wanted to remind you that I'm not the *only* one who would have wanted to be here twenty-four-seven to make sure you were okay."

He's talking about Dylan.

I nodded, blanketing over the statement. "I do spend a lot of time with those two, ever since Cheryl..."

His lips pushed together, eyes darting to the side to hide the uneasiness of mentioning Cheryl. "Yeah, I knew that," Jackson said. "So, do the hard thing, okay?"

My heart jumped into my throat, my eyes widening. It was exactly what I had said to him when I had walked in on him the first time he was hospitalized, a cord wrapped around his neck. "What did you just say?"

"I said do the hard thing. You don't like other people taking care of you. Do the hard thing in this situation and just let us be here for you, okay?"

I nodded, checking his face for any signals that he was provoking me.

"I'll see you later, Pippa. Let me know if you need anything." He disappeared, getting lost in the hustle of doctors and nurses outside my door. I exhaled, slow and steady into the center of the room, when Meg walked in with a vase full of flowers.

"Oh good, you're practicing your Lamaze. When are you due?"

"Very funny," I said, not opening my eyes. "Rough day, how's yours?"

"Just another day in paradise," she said, slugging her Burberry onto the chair next to the bed. What's new in recovery land?"

"Good news is it's going to rain later."

"Mmmmm yeah, I do adore a gray, soggy sky."

"When else is it acceptable to sit in the bottom of the shower with a beer if it's not raining?"

"Tuesdays, mostly," Meg said. She pretended to look under the hospital bed. "And where are you keeping the beer?"

"You mean you didn't bring any?"

"Negative, friend. I am rooting for full functionality of your brain before we ingest the liquid of the Gods again."

"Oh, so never then."

"Funny. You're feeling better then? You got your Pippa-tude back."

"Just another day in paradise," I repeated. "And since when do you give flowers?"

Meg looked at the vase in her hand like it was an alien. "Oh, I don't. The nurse practically threw them at me to bring them in here for you. It says they're from Dylan. Do you even like these flowers? They're pretty ugly. Reminds me of the ones I would get in high school."

"Eh, it's the thought that counts. Ohhhh, that explains the nurse's stares then."

"What?"

"Nothing," I said, not having the strength to rehash the story.

Meg flipped her auburn hair to the left and crossed her legs, reclining in her seat as she cleared her throat.

"Uh-oh," I said. "I'm going to get a *serious* talk, aren't I?"

She smiled. "You know me too well, friend. Does he know yet?"

"Jackson?"

"Yes. Does he know?"

"Does he know he's a functioning angerholic? Yes, I believe he's aware."

Meg rolled her eyes in response. "Does he know how you really met."

"Would it hurt or help?" I asked. "If he doesn't remember anyway, I don't see the point in hurting him and bringing it up now." It felt grimy projecting Jackson's opinion of a similar situation to Meg, but I wanted to know how she'd feel about it, being on the outside of everything.

"*You'd* know," Meg said. "And that's the worst person to know the truth, because one drunken night with Captain Morgan and Jackson in the same room will make your lips flap harder than a birds wings."

"I don't want to hurt him," I whined.

"You'll hurt him more by not telling him and he finds out. It's not fair, Pippa. I know you know that."

I nodded. "I do."

"Why do you care so much anyway?" she continued. "The last I got to peek at your desolate heart you were turned inside out about Dylan. You were talking about the possibility of you two getting back together and nagging me about if I would see him at the bar. You can't *save* Jackson, you can't fix him," Meg continued, her voice softening.

"I never wanted to fix him," I shot back, feeling resentment build inside of me.

Meg's eyes widened at the same time a sly smile started to turn the corners of her mouth upward. "Does that mean you..."

"It means I don't spend time with him because I feel like I need to fix him. You don't know him like I do, he's a savagely intricate person, almost to a fault."

"Almost to a fault," Meg repeated with sarcasm, her eyes dreamy.

"He has a really great heart, he really sees me."

"He *sees* you."

"And... and I..."

"And you...?" Meg pressed.

I sat there in silence, having a mental tantrum and shooting darts at Meg with my eyes. "And I think I'm tired, so this play date is over."

I rolled over on my side, my back facing the door. Meg said nothing and stood up, scraping her chair slowly across the floor to draw out the stall tactic she was trying to play.

"Pip?" I heard her say when she reached the door.

"Mmmmm?" I replied.

"Tell him. If you won't, then I will, and you know I will. He deserves to know that you've seen his worst parts and didn't run away screaming. That's important to some people, you know."

The door clicked behind her before I had a chance to answer and I lulled myself to sleep by clicking the morphine drip to its maximum dosage.

A few hours later I stirred in my sleep, feeling fingers clasped around mine in the bed. I tried not to smile at their warmth and the firmness that kept my fingers interlocked in place, safe and protected.

I took a few deep breaths. There was no part of me that wanted to hurt Jackson more than he already was, but I also knew Meg was right and that it would only be a matter of time before he found out if I kept it to myself. He deserved to know.

My lips parted and I squeezed his hand in mine, readying myself for the worst possible reaction but hoping for the best.

I opened my mouth and eyes at the same time, only to see Dylan slumped over the edge of my bed fast asleep, his hand entangled with mine. The rise and fall of his back told me he wouldn't see the look of disappointment on my face when I realized it was him.

Jackson saw it, though.

And I saw his.

A heart wrenching, confused expression crossed his face as he stared at me from the hospital room door, glancing from Dylan to my hand, then to my face. He stood motionless at the door, a bouquet of Slim Jims in one hand and my favorite flavor of Gatorade in another. I had no idea how long he had been standing there, watching us both sleep.

All at once it made sense. Dylan must have been there more than I remembered, looking over me as I recovered. At the same time, Jackson had been visiting, baffling the nurses about who was caring for me. As they tried to piece together who they were supposed to be addressing as my significant other, both Jackson and Dylan unknowingly rotated in and out of my hospital room like two ships passing in a fog.

I was the fog.

Keeping them both anchored by the choices I made, they both floated nearby with no real destination on the docket— my lies were impacting everything and everyone around me.

Jackson didn't say a word.

Lowering the Slim Jims to his side, he stepped backward. I watched him through the large windows that funneled into the hospital's hallway. Making a mad dash to the elevators, he only broke focus momentarily to leave the Slim Jims and Gatorade at the nurse's station outside my room.

Chapter 11

In the weeks that followed, I weighed the prognosis of my recovery based on the volume and frequency of the visits I got. They were dwindling, so I knew the critical period had passed and the recovery to make sure I regained all previous functions had begun. I was in the hospital just shy of two weeks, making the drive back home with Meg as soon as the doctors cleared me.

Jackson texted me a few times once I was home—testing the waters. His cryptic messages hinted at everything from wanting to stop by and check up on me to vulnerable defeat. Like me, he wanted to dissipate into the background noise of everything that happened until there was a definitive plan to what we were doing. It felt like we were stuck in this confusing, alternate universe. His short fuse distracted me from exploring a deeper relationship, but I was also privy to why he acted the way he did. Any time I was alone with my thoughts, though, I would second-guess my perceptions of who he was and how we met and the indiscretion of it all would crumble any aspirations I had to text him back.

So I never did.

I monitored television coverage of the Boston Marathon trials very closely. Many days I succumbed to the exhaustion or frustrations of only having one ear I could fully hear out of. Some days the ringing in my ear would be so loud, I'd turn the TV up to its max to drown out the sounds.

There were rallies outside of the courthouse, which was on Courthouse Way in Boston. Protestors were there, suggesting that the one terrorist was only an impressionable nineteen-year-old who had succumbed to his brother's wishes to plant the bomb. There were other opinions—after learning that he was responsible for placing the bomb on the pavement behind a group of kids, killing an 8-year-old boy— that he would need to be sentenced to death. Charges, including use of a weapon of mass destruction and the killing of an MIT police officer, loomed overhead. Only time would tell what his sentence would be.

Boston rallied with an uprising of inspirational slogans immediately after: 'Boston Strong', 'A Come-Together Moment', 'I Stand With Boston'. Rows of sneakers lined the streets, with art and photography awareness campaigns at the forefront of every magazine and newspaper headline.

It was the terrorist attack no one wanted to forget.

The devastation was too close to home.

The lives lost were too innocent.

Too much was taken.

That's how I felt standing near the nurse's station on my first day back at work. Getting cleared to come back on light duty required a few mental health tests, some additional scans and a few talks to the hospital higher ups who were truly compassionate about giving me all the time in the world to recover. They probably would have put me back on full duty if I had really pushed for it, but I was still fighting off bouts of dizziness from surgery, something the doctors said would be typical as I continued to recover.

Wanting something to focus on, I followed all protocols to get back to work as soon as I was able—taking only two weeks personal leave after returning home from the hospital.

Perhaps that was a mistake.

Part of me wondered if a portion of my face or skull had disappeared without me knowing it as I walked down the halls. The stares I got from co-workers in my unit were uncanny. The whispers in the hallways were undeniably loud: *Pippa had a relationship with a patient, a mentally unstable patient, a patient who needed her medical knowledge not her tongue down his throat.*

Surprised that my boss hadn't mentioned any ethics violations upon giving me my first shift schedule, I started to wonder if the rumors had reached her desk at all.

Until the end of my first day, anyway.

"Pip? Miss Grant asked to see you the end of your shift," Becca said, eyeing my face as she delivered the news.

"What for?" I asked sweetly, wanting her to voice the concern out loud for everyone to hear.

"Not sure," Becca said, shrugging. "I'm just the delivery person."

I took my time filling out the last of my paperwork at the end of my day, hoping the time that lapsed was enough to find she had gone home before meeting with me. I approached her office door, a soft light radiating from underneath it and I sighed, realizing I had no such luck.

I knocked.

"Pippa! I hope your first day back wasn't too overwhelming, how did it go?" Miss Grant said as I opened the door, peering inside. "Please, come in and sit."

"It was fine, Miss Grant. Same old, same old," I said.

"Please, call me Joanne. We're after hours at this point," she said winking, moving out from behind her desk to sit on the mahogany edge in front of the chair I was in. She crossed her ankles, revealing the telltale red bottomed heels that were her signature accessory.

She could stand on her feet for twenty hours a day and she wouldn't be caught dead without those heels. I respected her for her commitment to consistency. She wanted to present herself—at a hospital full of mostly male counterparts—in a very specific way. Always poised and professional, she emitted this aura of superiority that forced you to take her seriously. Even if she were telling us to put rubber ducks in every patient's toilet, we'd nod our heads and somehow justify it as we obliged. She always had the greater good of the hospital at the forefront of her mind and a reason for every powerhouse move she made, no matter how odd it seemed.

"I heard some things Pippa, some disturbing things. I think you know that, so I wanted to bring you in here to have a frank discussion about it so we can resolve the rumors floating through the halls."

"What kind of rumors?" I asked, wondering if she would humor me.

"Let's not," she replied, tipping her head. "I have a dinner I'm already late to, aching feet, and a bath calling my name later tonight. Let's put it all out there, shall we?"

"Jackson?" I asked, playing her game.

She nodded. "Jackson."

"What would you like to know?" I swallowed, wondering if I was truly ready to be fired.

Squinting, she looked past my shoulder, noticing the door to her office was open. She glided over, pushing it gently as she turned around to return to her spot on the edge of the desk. "Honestly? I don't want to know anything. That makes me an accessory to knowledge I'd rather not be a part of, do you see? Pippa, you're my strongest employee in the unit, you know that, I don't want to have this discussion any more than you do. I have an obligation to follow up with all ethical rumors that get dumped onto my desk, though, so humor me in telling me what you think I *should* know."

I nodded, understanding her position but also angry that any of my co-workers would think it necessary to bring the rumors to her attention to begin with. Unless, of course, they were vying for my job. A majority of the scheduling was based on seniority and how much the Nurse Manager tolerated you. I was fortunate enough to have both things on my side, allowing me for a fairly reasonable schedule as far as working as a nurse at a hospital goes. I knew Lisa wouldn't have snitched on me, but it would have been nearly impossible to keep Jackson's charts all to herself for the time he was admitted. I knew it would only be a matter of time before someone connected his delirious cries to me.

"The truth is..." I started.

Jacob barged in the door in that moment. "Boss, we have an emergency."

"My gosh Jacob, can't you see that—"

"There's a man in the emergency room from the prison, he shanked a guard and hit a nurse in the face, she's unconscious. The prisoner ran into a kid trying to escape and the father is threatening to sue for his injuries, it's an animal house down there."

"Oh, can't there just be *one* day," Joanne said, pinching the bridge of her nose. "I'll be down in a moment."

Jacob nodded—eyes wider than a softball—and closed the door behind him. His footsteps echoed down the hallway as he ran back to the E.R.

"Okay Pippa, let's fast track this. Do you have an ongoing relationship with this Jackson character?"

I opened my mouth, ready to defend myself and why he was in my life. That's when I realized he no longer was.

"I haven't seen him in weeks," I said out loud, the heaviness of the truth resting like an elephant on my chest. The last time I saw Jackson was when he left the hospital, Dylan's hands entangled in mine. A mixture of emotions from the attack, the betrayed look on his face that day, and a realization I may never be able to tell him the truth about us kept me from texting or calling him afterwards.

"Perfect!" Joanne said, raising her hands up as if to praise the hospital Gods. "If there's no relationship then the rumors I'm hearing are just rumors. Thanks for your time, Pippa. I need to get down to the emergency room, you may go."

I coasted down the hallway on autopilot, not caring that every co-worker I passed was staring at me to gauge how the meeting had went.

Thankful the staff locker room was mostly empty, I changed out of my scrubs and grabbed my jacket to head home.

I closed my eyes when the elevator doors closed, transporting to the lobby in solitude. Picturing Jackson's face on the last day I saw him, my heart ached, wondering where he was and what he had been up to. I had opened my phone, twice, to text him after coming home. I stared at the screen for so long that three familiar dots danced across the bottom at one point. Almost as if giving me my answer, nothing was sent, and I was left to wonder why it was so hard for him to talk to me when he needed to the most.

The doors beeped and I stepped out of the elevator, making my way to the front of the lobby.

"I thought you moved?" a voice called behind me, stopping me in my tracks.

When I turned Jackson was inches from my face with red cheeks, either from shock or panic, I couldn't tell.

"Jackson!" I yelled, alarmed at his presence, immediately thankful I had changed out of my scrubs. "You thought I moved?" I asked, not following.

"I went to your place, twice," he said. "You weren't there both times, your car gone, shades drawn. I drove past one night after work and it was completely black, I thought you up and moved."

"I've been staying with Meg temporarily," I answered. "She's been having a hard time with—" I looked around the lobby, the bustle of people around us telling me it wasn't the place or time to have heavy conversation. "She just needed a friend," I said, thinking about how our one-night sleepover had morphed into a long-term slumber party ever since I returned home. Neither of us wanted to be alone with our thoughts. "I planned to head home sometime next week."

"Oh, okay. Well...okay."

"What are you doing here?" he asked, scanning the lobby. "Are you okay?"

My face flared. "Just some follow up stuff, not a big deal." I tried to keep it vague. "What are *you* doing here?" I asked, looking around to see who was witnessing me talking to Jackson moments after telling my boss we had no contact.

"It's really nice to see you, Pippa" he said, ignoring the question entirely.

"Why? So you could remind me I was a terrible person for letting Dylan be there for me?"

"Don't be like that Pip, of course not. You needed everyone there for you. I needed to...I mean I wasn't sure if I should text you..." He looked away, his eyes searching in the space around us for any reason to run away. "I wanted to tell you..."

"Pippa?" said a voice directly behind me.

I stiffened, turning slowly, not wanting to face the reality of who it was.

Joanne smiled at Jackson warmly, but her face told me she was boiling with questions. "May I ask who your friend is? I'd love to be introduced."

I shook my head, not having a valid explanation and sensing in my gut that it would be the last time I would ever step foot in that hospital as an employee.

When I opened my mouth to respond, Jackson spoke over me.

"I was just asking where I could get a copy of my medical records." Jackson said smoothly.

I glanced from Jackson to Joanne, then back again. I wasn't sure what he was covering up, until I sensed a level of embarrassment in his voice. Taking notice of Joanne's professional getup, I think he assumed we were friends, not co-workers. He was trying to save me the embarrassment and complication of not knowing how to introduce him.

"I want to make sure my doctor has the most updated ones," he said.

Joanne nodded, not taking her eyes off Jackson. "Your doctor should know how to submit the request, no need to come to the hospital to get them Mr....?" She left the floor open for Jackson to provide his name, but he was skeptical of her digging. Reaching forward he extended his hand to her, shaking it when she offered hers, and then put his hand in his jean pocket.

"Perfect," he replied. He backed away, putting up a hand. "Again, sorry to waste your time." He was speaking directly to me, his eyes burning into mine, an agonizing look crossing his face. "It was never my intention to waste your time."

The gravity of his words lumbered at me like a sledgehammer. He nodded at Joanne, not bothering to look at me again as he started for the exit doors.

"Handsome man," Joanne replied, watching him disappear through the lobby. "If I didn't know any better, that'd be the elusive Jackson everyone is talking about. It doesn't look like he needs any medical attention and he never gave me his name though, so what do I know?"

I glanced at Joanne.

"It'd be a shame to lose your job over a rumor, wouldn't it, Pippa? I'm sure we won't see him here again," she cautioned.

My focus returned to a disappearing Jackson. I nodded, watching him walk away for the second time, this time not bothering to hide the quiver in my bottom lip.

. . .

Dylan had reappeared in my life just after the bombing, sporadically bringing me lunch at Meg's and keeping me company when he had the time. We poked fun of his nose brace and watched the news together, sometimes holding hands as the courthouse proceedings gave updates. I don't know if it was the thought of losing me that day, but something scared him into wanting me back in his life romantically. Somewhere around the three week mark of Jackson's absence and Dylan's overwhelming presence I told Dylan I needed space to focus on myself and so I could figure out was coming next.

The problem was, I had no idea what was coming next.

Chapter 12

"You're sure she had no idea I was gone?" I asked Meg, half heart-broken, merging onto the highway toward the nursing home.

Meg sighed through the Bluetooth call we were on, her voice hinting that she didn't want to go over it again. "Pip, I checked in on her once a week personally. We had tea together. She showed me her running sneakers, the purple comforter you gave her last Christmas and we talked about all sorts of things yes, but... none of those things was you, darling."

"So what did she talk about?"

"Soup, mostly. She said she wanted some soup that didn't taste like toilet water. Oh, and she asked if I could bring her to the beach."

"What'd you tell her?" I asked, nervous that she had become upset when Meg told her no.

"I told her sure, no problem. We'd go first thing after lunch."

I smiled. "You're a good friend."

"I knew she wouldn't remember by the time lunch rolled around. I didn't want to lie to her, but it was the happiest I saw her all day. If those few minutes were all she had to believe she'd be going to the beach, I'd lie to her over and over."

Meg was the kind of friend who knew how to give tough love when it was warranted, but she spent the weeks I was in the hospital looking after my mom without even asking if it was what I needed. It was never a question. She made sure the nurses knew that I was injured, and that she would be stopping in to check on her as often as she could.

She was a forever friend, the kind that implodes your heart with gratitude because you never knew how you survived before without them by the constant light they shined into your life.

"Thanks, Meg. So no mention of me?"

She sighed. "None. She did ask me to 'tell her one good thing and one bad thing', but I didn't know what that meant specifically."

I smiled, knowing that was Mom's way of shining through. "What'd you say?" I said, laughing.

"I told her the bad thing was I haven't been laid in a while, but the good thing was that it just meant that there was no way I could be pregnant."

"Meg!"

"Kidding!" she said, laughing. "I told her one good thing was I enjoyed having her to talk to, and one bad thing is I wish I could talk the same way with my sister again."

"You make my heart ache, woman."

"Yeah, well...time for me to go be a productive human being. You wanna binge on pizza and wine later? I've been in a funk and it's been a hot minute since we had a sleepover," Meg replied, deflecting.

"Is there any better way to spend a Sunday night?"

"Red or white?"

"Wine? Both, duh."

"You got it, see ya later."

I hung up with Meg as I pulled my car into a parking spot at the nursing home. The nurses at the front desk were happy to see me, and my heart quickened in anticipation of seeing my mom, whether she remembered me or not.

She was wrapped in her purple comforter when I poked my head through the door, an immediate smile lighting up her face.

"Hi there, stranger," I sang.

"Hi!" she said, pleased to have company regardless of who it was.

"Can I visit for a while?" I asked, pulling off my coat and setting it on the edge of her bed.

"Oh, I'd like that very much," she said, patting the bed beside her. "Can I get you some coffee? I just went grocery shopping today, I picked up this wonderful pumpkin roll."

Always worried about other people.

"I'm okay. Are you feeling all right?" I leaned forward, brushing a strand of white hair from her brow.

"Tulips," she said, staring at the batch I held in my hands.

I nodded, handing them to her.

She glanced at the flowers in her hands, turning them over and rubbing her fingers over the soft petals. Losing herself in this process, she looked up at me eventually and seemed surprised to see she had company. Her eyes darted from the flowers in her hand to me sitting on the bed beside her, and I could tell my presence of being so close to her when she didn't know who I was had her feeling uncomfortable. I stood up, slowly, and made my way over to the rocking chair a few feet away.

"Tell me one good thing and one bad thing," she said eagerly, straightening up in bed and readying herself for my reply, the tension from seconds earlier already forgotten.

I always thought it was amazing that she couldn't recall the important things: who I was, what year we were in, or even just remembering she was in a nursing home. Somehow, whether by repetition or some other unexplainable phenomenon, she would often remember to ask whoever was visiting the same question. It was a question she poised to me every day after school; then again when I was older, everyday after work or college classes. Maybe the things I deemed important that I wanted her to remember were selfishly only for me. She obviously remembered what she did for a reason, and I was still learning to accept that our ideas of what was important would be vastly different.

She taught me that if it was the end of the day and you couldn't identify a 'good thing', it meant you had to create your own good by doing something for someone else. Some days would have more good than bad things, more bad than good, or they would balance out. It was a checks and balances game she created for life to keep good things in the world revolving. She taught me that I should create some good for someone else when I couldn't see any good in my own life.

"My good thing for today is that I got to bring my mom flowers."

I would sometimes purposefully not call her Mom. Too many times the title gave her anxiety or confused her because she didn't know why I would be calling her that. It was easier to show up as a friend, just someone who wanted to talk and visit, rather than remind her over and over of who she forgot she was.

"Oh, I bet she loved that."

"She did," I said smiling at her. "She loves tulips, so she made me bring her flowers every Sunday to teach me to remember her at least once a week."

"Oh, well I think you should remember your mother more than once a week," she chastised, wagging a finger.

"I agree, and I do for sure. She wanted me to get into the habit of remembering her for when she wasn't here anymore. I would be so used to bringing her flowers on Sundays, I'd do it even when she was gone."

She nodded, staring at the tulips still clutched in her hand. "That's a lovely notion."

"It is."

There was a moment where it was silent, her fingers gently caressing the petals, when she looked up.

"And your bad thing?"

Surprised she remembered asking the question in the first place, I wiggled in my seat. "There's a lot of those lately, I almost don't know where to start."

"Mmmmm. Sounds like things are unbalanced."

"That's an understatement," I said, moving back to the bed to sit by her side, judging her face to make sure it was okay. "I've hurt someone without them knowing I've hurt them."

It was a gesture that made my heart turn as warm and soft as her hand felt, when she picked mine up and placed it in hers. "How have you hurt someone? Did you apologize?"

"There's nothing to apologize for because he doesn't even know I'm hurting him. I'm keeping something from him, a secret."

"Mmmmm," she said.

I wasn't sure if I had lost her in conversation again so I continued on. "He has been there for me more times than I deserve, but I never fully return the favor. I'm still hurting from what happened with Dylan, but now Jackson is paying for it. He should know more about me but I can't let him in. I'm too afraid."

Mom exhaled slowly and patted my hand. "Yes, I can tell you're afraid. You don't have to be afraid." She gave my hand a little squeeze, and even if her understanding of what I was saying was out of context it was exactly what I needed from her.

"What would you do about Jackson?" I asked.

Mom smiled. "Well, have you told him?"

"Told him what?"

"That you love him."

I was taken aback. Her perception of love sounded so normal, so easy. Maybe it was. Maybe loving someone wasn't based on the things they did or didn't do to prove it, but instead was weighed more by the void you felt when you weren't in their presence.

"No, Mom, I haven't. Wait, how did you—"

"I would tell Jackson that you love him, Pippa. Life is too short to not be with the one you love. When Roger flew off to Cambodia with you only two months grown in my belly I thought there was no way we could make it work if I just showed up to another country pregnant. Now I wish I had gone to him, who knows what kind of happiness I missed out on."

"Mom?" I asked, tears welling up in my eyes. "Do you really know who I am?"

"Of course I do, baby. And I'm sorry I made the decision for the both of us to miss out on Roger in your life, you didn't deserve that."

I threw my arms around her neck, sobbing into her hair. "Oh, Mom! Oh, I've needed you so bad…"

My shoulders shook and she patted my back. I was a child again, crying to my mother as though I had fallen off my bike. She patiently waited for my sobs to subside and pushed me away from her.

"I'm right here, Pippa. You're the best thing that ever happened to me. I hope you know that I'm always here."

I nodded as she turned to her nightstand. "Speaking of that, I want to do my 'something good' for the day," she announced. Reaching inside the drawer, she brought out a small, glass cylinder. She opened my palm and placed it inside, closing my fingers around it. "I want you to have this."

Bringing the vial up to my face, I turned it over in my hand, suddenly remembering my lunch with Meg from months ago when the same exact thing appeared on my lunch plate at The Inlet. "Mom, where did you get this? Who gave this to you?"

"I don't know, actually," she said pensively. "I just want you to have it."

"Why?"

"It's the beach," she said, pointing to the granules inside. "I am always so happy when I am at the beach and you look so sad. You can carry it with you, so you always have a bit of happy."

I smiled, patting the top of her hand, then bringing her hand up to my lips and kissing the back of her knuckles.

"Does this mean I did a good thing?" Mom giggled.

"It means you did the best thing," I replied.

"Will you visit with me for a while? I can make us some tea, and I might be able to find those cookies you like before you head back to college."

The bits and pieces that still were amiss in her memory while she was lucid were hard to listen to. "I'll stay as long as I possibly can," I assured her, pulling out my phone to text Meg that I was going to have to postpone our wine and pizza date.

MEG! She's lucid, staying as long as I can. Rain check for tonight?

She must have been sitting right by her phone, because her reply was almost instant.

OMG. Of course! Hug her for me. Tell her about Jackson.
Don't tell her about the bombing. Tell her everything.
HUG HER MORE. Then come home and tell me everything.
What I would give to talk to Cheryl right now. GO!
STOP READING MY RAMBLINGS OMG I LOVE YOU SO HAPPY FOR YOU.

I locked my phone after reading her text, a smile so wide across my face it made my cheekbones tingle. "Do you want to hear about how I met Jackson, Mom?"

"I'd love that," she replied. "But first...Pippa, can I ask you something?"

"Anything."

"Are we staying at a hotel?"

Chapter 13

J ust like Mom, I was half-asleep most of the time, drifting in and out of a fog.

Morning was my favorite time of day because it meant I had a brand new twenty-four hours to readjust my sails and attempt to re-ground myself. Breakfast would consist of an omelet, coffee, and searching current topics on my Twitter feed to assess the lives of celebrities I would never meet. I'd check emails and cross off checklists for paperwork that was backing up at work, then have to re-coffee.

Somewhere after the daily conference call or email exchange with my boss, I'd munch on some fruit or get lost in a text exchange with Meg about her latest dating drama or vent over her lack of ovaries from when endometriosis took them from her. I'd call the nursing home, but only after I watched funny videos from my phone that popped up on social media, because sometimes the news wasn't always sunshine and unicorns. Actually, news from the nursing home was mostly filled with updates of Mom's medications or whatever episodes she experienced the evening before that were worse than normal.

Usually after those calls, I'd get lost.

I'd find myself staring out the kitchen windows, looking for cardinals and surveying the modest acre of property from my one bedroom apartment. The quiet that surrounded me was unusual, at least to me, since I had come from a life-in-the-fast-lane that my career had provided up until the attack. Light duty meant half the hours, half the responsibility, and half the distraction I so desperately needed. The hum of my nearly dead refrigerator clinked in the background while I wasted time trying to find myself, trying to wake up.

The attack.

The explosion.

The accident.

The ending.

I had called it so many different things in my head for so long that I sometimes failed to see what it was in its true form; murder.

It was murder. My love of camaraderie running against the pavement with complete strangers nearly killed me.

And for what?

True to my personality, before I got too lost thinking about the 'what ifs' or 'if onlys', I pried myself away from the window, heading toward my bedroom.

I had to get out.

If I ran fast enough, the pounding in my head would fall into rhythm with the beats in my chest. If I ran far enough, the past would struggle to keep up, and it would float away from me, evaporating into the air like a morning fog rising off of the ocean.

I never did run fast or far enough.

I tried, though. I tried to forget Jackson barking catcalls from behind me about how the shape of my ass made him want to take me home instead of finishing the run. We would push each other to the edge of exhaustion, nodding in each other's direction in support when the playlist blaring through my ear buds set my pace just right and there was no room for talking between steps.

I ran alone now. The moment my doctor approved me for exercise, I was lacing up a pair of sneakers in an attempt to escape my own thoughts.

Jackson was a memory I was trying to live without. He had trained with me for weeks, sloshing through cold, sand, and rain just to help me get in one extra mile. I never explored why he was so dedicated and supportive, but retrospect is a funny thing. All the notions I had considered in the past about him maybe loving me and wanting to be by my side while I trained for the hardest marathon I would ever run in my life were long gone.

He was never training *for* me, I had concluded, he was training *with* me. His absence in my life was all the proof I needed to know he wasn't serious about keeping anything between us going.

I crossed Island Drive on the south side of Topsail Island, heading north. I knew that if I could just make it four more blocks I'd be able to turn around and call the day a success. My therapist had told me to increase my radius two blocks at a time.

"Is it the distance or pain that prevents you from getting to the beach?" she had asked. She poised her pen above her clipboard, anticipating my response. When I turned to gaze out the window instead of answering, she lowered the pen and sighed. "You can *tell me*, Pippa."

Rain had collected on the window in her office and I watched the beads of water drift into each other until they were so dense and unstable they'd slide uncontrollably down the glass. It was exactly how I felt most of the time. One minute I was standing at the corner waiting for a light to turn green so I could finish my run and the next I was fetal positioned on a bench outside of the Polish Deli, unable to breathe or move.

"Meg came and got me the last time," I said. "The store owner had to call her to come pick me up. I couldn't move." I kept my eyes transfixed on the raindrops, watching them spiral out of control to the bottom was comforting. It was like I wasn't alone. My eyes shifted to the light switch on the wall above my therapist's right shoulder.

She followed my gaze and her eyes softened. "I can turn the lights down a bit, if you want. Is it too bright in here still?"

The lights were half dimmed but I had worked so hard to not let my sporadic sensitivity to light overpower me, so I shook my head. "They're fine. I know it's safe here."

Bright lights. The smell of the pavement. Busy public places.

All triggers I was trying to manage.

"Yes, it is safe here, Pippa. So about the beach..."

"Jackson," I said. "He's the reason I can't get to the beach."

It was a bold statement. I had never mentioned his name in therapy before so she leaned forward with eager eyes at my disclosure.

"Who's Jackson, Pippa?"

I closed my eyes and let the question repeat itself several times in my head. *Who is he really? Who's Jackson? Where is he? Where did he go? WHERE IS HE?*

When I opened them to look at her, hot tears feverishly slid down both cheeks. Blinking them away wouldn't help, I knew that already, so I let them fall into my lap. "I don't know," I answered, finally.

Confused, my therapist sat in silence, waiting for me to continue.

"I don't know who he *is*," I admitted, looking at her. "I just know who he *was*."

My most recent therapy session echoed in my head as I crossed Harrison Street. A pink silhouette still hovered across the skyline. If I hurried, I could make two more blocks and be back home before the sun started to set.

Topsail Island was a twenty-six mile barrier island on the coast of North Carolina. I was lucky to have my mom, a career, the beach, and a hole in the wall bar I loved to go to with my best friend all within an hour drive away. It was fate that the marathon I had gruelingly trained and qualified for was exactly twenty-six miles.

As I made my way past Eighteenth Avenue, I tried to push thoughts of Jackson from my head. He was the one who convinced me that running twenty-six miles would be cake for someone who had run the hundreds of miles I logged each year. It was his persistence and eagerness to wake up at four a.m. everyday to train with me that led us to the morning of the scariest day of my life.

The day everything changed.

I cruised past the Polish Deli, thankful that the shop wasn't open yet so I didn't have to wave to the owner. He only remembered me as the woman who broke down on his stoop, the woman who started to hyperventilate so violently that I couldn't dial my phone. He only remembers me asking to go inside the shop, and screaming at him to turn out all the lights so I could sit in a dark corner to wait for Meg to rescue me. I could hear his saturated dialect try and calmly explain to Meg what was happening, in English, but I don't think he ever witnessed someone crash to rock bottom before.

And it wouldn't be the last time I did.

I jogged past Kent Avenue, a familiar tightening in my chest threatening to make me turn around. Keeping my momentum, I tried to focus on the reason I was pushing so hard.

"I did it, I finally qualified for this marathon," I had said to Meg, remembering back to when I first showed her my acceptance letter months before. "I have to train every day now. Oh, it's going to be so amazing. Cheering crowds and people running together in a sea of sweat, ugh I can't wait." I sat on the sofa, a carton of cookies-and-cream ice cream in my lap. "My diet should change a bit, I guess."

"A sea of sweat? *That* was your motivation to do a marathon?" Meg asked, stealing my spoon and helping herself to a mile-high bite.

"You want to be my motivation instead?" I teased. "Run with me. We can train together and when the day comes you can jump into the street so we can cross the finish line together. Wouldn't it be fun?"

"Fun, yup. Also, I think that'd be cheating. Also probably illegal, I think they have security people for that. *I* didn't qualify, *you* did," she said, rolling her eyes.

"Wait, Pip?"

"Yeah?" I said between mouthfuls of food.

She cocked her head to one side. "What marathon did you qualify for again? I forget. The ass-growing one?" Her eyes shifted to the spoon I had poised at the opening of my mouth, a mound of ice cream haphazardly teeter tottering on the edge.

"Boston," I said, grinning ear to ear. "On April 15th I'll be running the Boston Marathon."

"You happy about that?"

"Not at all," I said exhaling, my cartoon-grin forcing a smile to spread across Meg's face. "I am the most unhappy runner in the world today."

A car horn shook me from the daydream I had immersed myself in. I stumbled backward onto the curb, the front bumper of the car grazing my leg.

"Crazy! Get off the road!" the man from the passenger seat shouted through the window.

My hand found its place on my chest as I sucked in gasps of air, all focus starting to crumble. I put my hands on my hips and looked around for a distraction as my breaths started to become more rapid.

You're fine, you're fine.

Where are you?

How far are you?

I talked to myself as my eyes locked on a street sign that read FIFTH AVENUE. "You're at Fifth Avenue?! You're almost at the beach. You almost did it. "

The sun hugged the skyline, flooding light onto the sidewalk and streets for one last hurrah before it started its descent. The ground swayed beneath me as I struggled to balance my breathing and instinctively I reached for my phone. Dropping to my knees I opened my text messages, fighting with myself to decide whether or not I needed to ask Meg to come get me.

"Why am I like this," I whispered, staring at Jackson's name several messages down.

My phone was a vault of memories. When you care about someone and don't realize it's the last time you'll ever speak to them, you tend to hold onto emotional memorabilia longer than you should. Those messages were the only memories I had left. I could revisit them anytime I wanted, to remind myself that he was real and that he could have been so much more than a running buddy if I had put my selfishness aside.

I scanned over Dylan's name and opened up Jackson's instead. Our last text was ancient, it was practically mummified sitting among conversations I had with other people who texted me on a regular basis.

The impact of staring at Jackson's name in my phone was immediate.

My breaths slowed, and the ground stopped swaying so hard. I tried to blink the focus back into my eyes. As I sat staring at the last thing we wrote to each other, the bottom left corner of our conversation started to move.

I knew what was happening. I had opened up our conversation millions of times. I had typed messages out every once in a while, only to delete it. Still, I couldn't believe what I was seeing.

The bottom showed three round bubbles, each one filling up in succession, a gratifying occurrence when someone was typing a reply to a text message. I stared at the screen, breathless, waiting for them to stop and for words to appear in our conversation. I waited to see what had Jackson texting me at that exact moment, with me kneeling on the side of Fifth Avenue battling a past I was trying to outrun.

They continued pulsing like a heartbeat that was shocked back to life. They danced while my inhales and exhales slowed to a normal rhythm.

Without thinking twice about it, I texted Jackson the GPS location of where I was kneeling and nothing more. His reply was immediate:

I'll be there in two minutes.

I didn't need to explain anything.

I navigated to a nearby bench, bringing my knees to my chest and dropping my head in my hands. It seemed like a century before Jackson's car pulled up to the curb. His dashboard reflected only a nine-minute lapse of time from the text I sent him.

We sat in silence, his car weaving traffic like a seal explores the ocean. I don't know how I knew he would bring us to the beach but I was relieved when we pulled into our usual meeting spot. He opened his door after finding a parking spot, ran around front, and opened my door.

The cool sand that was cast in shadows from the buildings on the shoreline flicked my ankles as he pulled me onto the beach. My hand enclosed in his, I followed, succumbing to his silent guidance like a lost child at a parade.

When we got to the water's edge he spun around and sat down in the sand, gently tugging on my hand to follow him. He removed my shoes and socks, then his own. Placing his hand over mine, he scooped up handfuls of sand and placed them into my palms, coaxing my hands to transition it from one hand to another in a platonic game of don't-spill-the-sand.

I was transfixed.

I was also finally cognizant of what had just happened.

"How am I supposed to go on like this?" I said finally, letting the last handful of sand rejoin its place on the ground in front of me.

"Like what?" His voice was like velvet, soothing me in a way I didn't know I needed.

"Like *this*," I said, lifting my chin for the first time to look him in the face.

He nodded, but the tear streaming down his left cheek did not go unnoticed. "The same way I do," he said.

"How's that? How do you just go on living like you haven't been through the worst thing in your life? At what point can I control these anxiety attacks instead of letting them steam roll over me when I least expect it? How will this ever work?"

"With each other," he said, confidently. "I don't *need* you Pippa, I'm a grown man and I own all my choices. I can't fix the parts of me that ruptured because my parents died or because I saw too much fighting a war for my country that I didn't start. I *want* you, Pip. I want to spend time around someone who trusts me enough to text me their location and know I'll show up. I'm not trying to be un-broken, I would just rather be broken with you. You're the only one who understands how I feel."

"Would we really want that? It sounds like a recipe for disaster."

"I do, I wouldn't say it if I didn't."

"So what, we pretend we're not kneeling in the middle of streets or needing to be coaxed out of panic attacks with beach sand? We just hold onto each other and fall apart?"

"It's a start," he said, grabbing my hand. "After all, when you were at your lowest just now, who did you text?"

I stared at him, not wanting to admit that I was aching for him too. He was right. When I was at the peak of an anxiety attack, Jackson was the first person I wanted to call. I think crisis situations and good news always help identify who is truly important in your life. When something terrible or wonderful happens, there's always that *one* person that you want to tell first.

My person just happened to have been MIA since I returned home from the hospital.

"So if that's how you feel where have you been, Jackson?"

His mouth twitched. "I was waiting for you to figure out where I fit. You called me today, though, so maybe I now I know. Look, I've been meaning to give you something..."

"It's not enough," I whispered, cutting him off.

"If you need more help we'll find it. Give it over to me Pip, let me carry some of this with you. We can—"

"I wasn't talking about you," I whispered, turning my face to the ocean. "I meant it's not enough for my daughter, Jackson. *I'm* not going to be good enough."

The words fell out of my mouth. I didn't intend on saying them, but there was no other way for me to describe the gravity of how I felt. He needed to know the truth.

"Your...daughter?" Jackson asked.

I shrugged, unable to look him in the face. "Surprise," I said, annoyed at the burning in my chest. "Her name is Phoenix. I guess we're both not who we needed each other to be."

"How? I mean, who do you have a —?" He stopped, his eyes darkening at the realization that he knew the answer before I had a chance to tell him. "Dylan?"

I nodded.

The silence was deafening, even over the roar of the ocean. The crunch of the particles of sand between his fists was all I could focus on. He stared at the waves hitting the shore before standing to his feet.

When I was finally able to look at him I could see the wheels turning, but he said nothing.

"Say something," I demanded.

"There's nothing for me to say," he said, twisting the tip of his toe into the sand. He sighed, sucking his chest inward, then he turned and started to walk away. "I need to go."

He got about five feet away when a rage I didn't know I even had forced my mouth open. "You're not even going to ask?! You don't even want to know any of the backstory? Nothing? You can just walk away from what I just told you, just like that?!" I screamed after him.

"It doesn't matter," he called over his shoulder plainly, his back still to me.

"No, of course it doesn't matter," I wailed. "It never matters once a kid is involved right?! I'm damaged goods as far as you're concerned huh? Well here's the kicker, Jackson, just because I said I *have* a kid with Dylan doesn't mean I *had* a kid with Dylan. She's not mine by blood, not that it matters. She's *my daughter* because I raised her from the time she was born and I love her more than life itself. Not that you'd have any clue about what that means!"

I struck a nerve. Jackson looked over his shoulder and I could feel the corners of his eyes staring me down in his peripherals. He still refused to turn around.

"We were on a break, me and Dylan," I said, tears refusing to stay at bay any longer. "I was feeling sorry for myself and wound up at a bar talking to some woman who was there keeping an eye on her younger sister who had a history of making really awful choices once she was out of the military."

Dylan turned around, and we stood facing each other five feet apart, my fists shaking with adrenaline.

"Meg?" Jackson said, watching tears fall from my cheeks to my chin.

"Meg," I repeated. "That's the night I met her. The night we became best friends. That's when Dylan walked into the same bar, a complete and freak coincidence."

"Phoenix is Meg's baby?" Jackson mouthed.

I shook my head. "No, Jackson. Phoenix isn't Meg's baby. Dylan showed up half lit as it was, but it took him two beers and a shot of Jim Beam to realize I was sitting at the other end of the bar. He left, and Meg and I didn't see him the rest of the night."

"So who...?"

"Meg's sister Cheryl was outside smoking a cigarette when he stormed out. She used him as her getaway car since she was tired of being under the watch of a babysitter. Ultimately the cab only had one stop that night. Dylan had no intentions of seeing her again after that night. I kept in touch with Meg because we bonded that night. We were both heartbroken, me about Dylan and her about Cheryl. I found out Cheryl was pregnant a few weeks later when Meg and I reconnected to go out for her birthday and some drinks. That's when she told me and we put the timeline together. I drunk dialed Dylan from the bar that night and told him that Cheryl was pregnant. Dylan didn't plan to get someone pregnant while we tried to work out where our relationship was headed. After the initial shock wore off Dylan and I *did* get back together. Cheryl was still pregnant when we got back together, so I've been there for Phoenix since the very beginning."

Jackson's eyes appeared to quiver, but he blinked and ran his hand through his hair instead. "I didn't know, Pip..."

"You never gave me a reason to tell you!" I yelled at him. "You never made me feel that it was important enough to tell you because I was always too busy taking care of *you*. Worrying about *you*."

"What's that supposed to mean?"

"I'm always taking care of everyone else. Cheryl made it two months clean after Phoenix was born before old habits crept in. She did the right thing and remained clean her whole pregnancy but she couldn't cope with her PTSD and a new baby. She overdosed just before Phoenix was three months old. I watched Dylan and Meg grieve with the fallout and I rushed in to love a baby who didn't ask for any of it. I convinced Dylan to let me co-parent her with him, for better or for worse, they both needed me."

"So you're married?" he said, swallowing the words like a golf ball.

"No, Jackson. We can co-parent without being married. I couldn't blame him for the baby, especially since I was the reason why we had taken a break in the first place after years of being together. It never would have happened otherwise...but I'm the only mom she's ever known. She's three now but Dylan and I split for the last time when she was around two years old. I still take her every chance I get. Meg and I do a damn good job making sure she's the center of our universe. Dylan and I are trying our best to balance it all since we're not together."

"Why did you break up?"

"You don't get to ask that now. You just tried leaving, just like every other guy who finds out I'm helping to raise a baby that isn't mine with my ex. How do you think that would go over on a first date? Maybe I should though, I'm certainly not ashamed of her like I am of people like you who think it's a good reason to walk away."

"Pip, tell me, why did you break up?" His eyes were desperate. Shifting his weight from one foot to the other he crossed his arms over his chest. He didn't move toward me, but I felt a magnetic tug eerily pulling us closer.

"He didn't see me," I said. My chest heaved, remembering the night I told Dylan to leave. "At some point he stopped seeing me. When I walked into a room, when I smiled at him, anytime I made an effort to look my best or go out of my way to make him feel special... he never saw me. I was ghosted but still in a relationship. So I *really* disappeared, I left him, so he could see what it would be like without me. It backfired."

"I see you."

I stared at him, my heart thrashing as he retraced his steps and closed the gap between us. He pulled on my chin with one hand when we reached me, forcing me to look at him.

"I see you. I do." He opened my right palm with his free hand, never breaking eye contact, and dropping something cold and rectangular in the center.

"What's this?"

"And, like I said before," he said keeping my attention. "None of what you said matters and there's nothing else for me to say. I need to go. Call Meg to come get you."

My chin remained frozen in its upright position as Jackson let his hands fall to his sides. I opened my mouth as he turned his back to me, but nothing came out. It was almost slow motion, watching him reach the dunes and crossing over them. He pulled a small, blue box from his pocket and chucked it into the dune grass, disappearing into the distance and leaving me with only the howl of the ocean winds to comfort me.

He left.

Again.

I told him the darkest, most vulnerable pieces of me and he walked away from them like he was leaving a coffee shop. Water welled up in both of my eyes as I clenched both of my fists. The cold metal tingling on the inside my right hand forced me to look down.

Through the blur of tears I could see two dog tags on a chain, each with a one-word inscription engraved on the back.

Before. & *Always.*

Chapter 14

our weeks.

That's how long Jackson and I played the game of making bubbles pop up on each other's screens. I would write an entire, hate-filled paragraph and delete it all moments before hitting send.

I would go into work, still on light-duty, and find a bathroom stall between seeing patients. Utilizing talk-to-text I'd mind-dump every salty thought I had with fervor, then clear the message before leaving the bathroom.

Watching the bubbles pop up on my screen was infuriating.

I had no idea why he bothered keeping my number in his phone at all with how our last encounter ended.

I wound up sitting on the beach in a stupor that day, before finally calling Meg to come get me. She spent the next couple of hours letting me cry my mascara off, blackening her shirt.

Meg's way of comforting someone would be to pat them with a broom from a few feet away. I knew I was in a state of hysteria considering she practically let me ruin the blouse she had on that day. She also fed me copious amounts of rum and ginger ale—again—like a true friend would.

The next morning I woke up puffy-eyed but refreshed. I felt like I shed a skin that had been dangling from my ankles. For two weeks after the fight I dove head first into consuming any of my free time with work, albeit light-duty responsibilities drove me insane, just to pass the time.

I spent more time with Phoenix than I had in the past year combined, taking her to every park within a twenty mile radius more times than I could count.

Meg joined me at the gym more than ever. Unsure if she was doing it out of guilt or a newfound love of fitness, I'd remind her she didn't have to hover over me like I was lost.

"You were right," I said, more assured than I was willing to admit. "I let my own selfishness put a blindfold over me and the whole situation with Jackson."

"I often am right, love," Meg said on the treadmill next to me.

"So what do I do now? It doesn't hurt any less," I admitted.

Meg nodded, her cheeks flustered. "You do what everyone else in our situation does. You do what Phoenix has to do when we take her to visit Cheryl's grave. You do what I have had to do every day since Cheryl killed herself. You do what Dylan does now that he finally realizes the magnitude of what he lost by not appreciating you, and you do what your mom does every single morning."

"What's that?"

She wagged a finger at me. "You keep fucking going."

The second half of the month was easier. Running was back in my routine on a daily basis and I was visiting my mom more. By the end of the month, I gave Joanne my blessing to put me back on the schedule full-time. I was chugging along, fairly certain that I was making productive strides forward.

Then, I made the mistake of visiting Meg at The Inlet.

"You *do* exist," Meg said, wide-eyed when I sat down. "I thought you'd joined the ranks of Santa Claus and the Tooth Fairy, rarely seen but mysteriously real."

"One *very* strong Long Island, bartender," I said, motioning with a finger to the empty coaster in front of me. "Pronto. Plus, don't give me that, it's literally been four days since I saw you last."

"Oh boy, you're having a sleepover at my house tonight aren't you? I can feel it."

"Good possibility," I said, eyeing her hands as she poured my drink to life.

"That's called enabling though, isn't it?" she chimed in.

"I call it you get free entertainment since you're at work and can't drink anyway, so don't complain."

Meg pulled a styrofoam cup up onto the counter from behind the bar. "Coffee's for the weak," she said, winking.

"Rum?"

"Rum, coffee, they're both dark and alter the tolerance level you have for other people so it's win-win."

"You're daring. Doing that often?"

"Only days that end in 'Y' lately."

I nodded. "To your coffee."

"To your liver," Meg said, tipping the coffee cup to her mouth.

We both smiled as we brought our cups to the counter.

There was some tension. Meg opened her mouth to say something, but covered it up by coughing. I did the same, wanting to speak but instead pretending I was fishing a random piece of something out of my back tooth instead.

"Oh God, you're going to ask me," Meg said, the moment of silence lasting too long.

"Ask you what?"

"No, the answer is no Pippa. I won't do it."

"Do what?!"

"I'm not feeding into this, the woe-is-me thing you're doing right now. Don't you dare ask me about him."

"Who?"

"Oh myyyyy..." Meg said, putting her hands up to the sides of her face. "I can't believe that even if I saw him you'd want me to tell you anything about him."

"You're supposed to be my best friend."

"That is never argued, however, you coming in here for an *innocent* drink without asking me if Jackson has been here is noted."

"He keeps doing the three dots thing, he just won't hit send."

"Have you?"

"No," I scoffed. "Why should I? He's the one who walked away."

"So why bother wondering then?"

"Because...because obviously I just..." I shrugged, taking another sip of my drink for a pause. "I just would want to know..."

"There's nothing to know, Pip. He hasn't been here. In fact he hasn't been anywhere. Of course I'm your best friend, but I haven't seen him."

I swallowed. "I know. I went to his apartment building."

"Pippa!"

"I had to see for myself how he was doing without me. I wanted to watch him walk out of his building in the morning with a coffee cup in one hand and a smile on to know I was justified in not reaching out to him."

"And...?"

"He never came out. He didn't come out the next day, or the next..."

"Okay stalker, how many days did you—"

"Just three. Then I asked the doorman. Jackson moved, Meg. He up and left."

"Maybe his lease was up?" she suggested.

"He didn't leave a forwarding address but paid for the month in full before leaving."

"Maybe he was planning to move out regardless of what happened between you two?"

"The doorman said he moved out on the same day we fought on the beach."

"Woah."

"Yeah. I was hoping maybe he just...moved somewhere else or something."

"Well, he did, clearly."

"Somewhere else around *here*."

"I'm sorry," Meg offered.

"Maybe you could call him quick?"

"Pippa Winters! You know my rule."

"You can pretend he left something here and just ask where to forward it to."

"That's some true crime TV level shit, Pippa. I don't call people from the bar, especially to come meet up with your level of crazy. Let's just make that clear as glass."

"Do it for me."

"What about Dylan?"

"What about him?" I said.

"Yow, watch the sass lady, I was just asking as a concerned friend."

"Sorry," I mumbled.

"Accepted. So what about Dylan? Where does he fit in all of this?" A patron waved at Meg from down the bar, to which Meg held up a finger motioning for him to wait a minute. "A regular, never mind him. Please continue."

"He fits like a puzzle piece."

Meg heightened her left eyebrow. "And that means...?"

"He fits right where he should, it works, but the slightest movements pull us apart again."

"Deep," Meg said, nodding. "You should write that one down."

"You should do your job before you get fired," I said, sweetly waving at the patron down the bar who was growing impatient.

"Worth it," Meg said. "You know, what you and Dylan have is complicated but he does love you. I know you love him. That doesn't mean you have to be together. You'll always do the right thing for Phoenix, that's never a concern. So maybe you need to figure out what's right for you."

"Phoenix," I said, rolling her name over on my tongue. "Crazy, the irony of her name, isn't it?"

"A mythical bird that is born from the ashes. I think about it all the time," Meg admitted. "She's grown from the ashes of so much heartache." She exhaled, bringing her chin to her chest. "Okay, session's over for today. I'll bill you, so leave your address with my receptionist. I have goose bumps." She smoothed the hairs on her left arm.

"Thanks, Dr. Phil." I pulled my phone out of my pocket that had started to vibrate. "Now go away, I have drinking and self-loathing to do."

Meg curtsied in front of me and then walked to the end of the bar.

"Pippa," I said, picking up the call.

"Miss Winters? This is Mrs. Frye calling. Do you have a moment?"

My heart dropped. "My mom...?"

"She's fine! Totally fine, please forgive me if I startled you by calling in the evening. I know you usually call in the mornings for her progress updates."

I exhaled slowly, motioning Meg away with my hand since my wide eyes while on the call magnetized her in my direction. 'It's okay' I mouthed, and she went back to putting orders up on the bar, narrowing her eyes at me.

"Sure, what's going on?"

"Some good news. I know we always don't have the happiest of things to share so I wanted to reach out personally. Your mom has been responding so well to the gentleman who has been coming to visit her, I know sometimes she can get confused with who people are but he really has a way of opening her up and keeping her happy. I'm sure you'd want to know that we encourage anything that makes our residents' stay more comfortable and enjoyable."

I thought of Dylan's name still being registered on her emergency call list and what Meg and I had just talked about. "I agree," I said. "Speaking of that, is there any way I'd be able to move someone from my mom's emergency contact list to just their visitor list?" I didn't want to pull his visitor rights if it made Mom happy, but I also wanted to set some boundaries.

"Certainly, let me pull up her file."

I could hear a burst of clicks and taps on the other end. "Ah, here we go. Who would you like to remove from the emergency list?"

"Dylan."

"Very good. And you want me to keep him on the visitor list?"

"Please," I said, swirling the straw in my drink and watching the ice clink off the glass, feeling an odd sense of closure and resolution with the decision.

"All right, very good. You're all set. I'm assuming given our conversation you'd want me to keep visitor access open to the volunteer group that works through your hospital?"

"Oh, yes, that's fine."

"Excellent. Jackson has really helped make her weeks a little brighter. Not many volunteers are able to come in here and bring a story to life the way he does and you can tell she really enjoys it. Speaking of, he just arrived! Let me go help sign him in. Thanks again, Pippa, we'll talk in the morning."

Meg rushed in front of me before I could hang up the phone. "Why is your face like that? Pip, why is your mouth open? What's going on?"

"I have to go," I said, shoving my phone into my pocket and throwing a twenty onto the bar.

"Wait, are we still having a sleepover? I could use one. What's going on!"

"Sure, I'll explain later. Bring my Long Island with you," I demanded.

"Pip!"

"I know where Jackson is!" I called over my shoulder, pushing through the doors to the outside deck and practically sprinting to my car.

Chapter 15

"**P**ippa! We weren't expecting you, is everything—"

I rushed past the reception desk at the front of the nursing home, barreling toward my mom's room without saying a word.

"Okay! Well, we'll just sign you in and…"

The voice trailed behind me. I don't know who was more startled when I opened the door, my mom or Jackson.

Mom placed her hand over her heart when the door flew open. Jackson dropped the book he was reading onto the bed, putting an arm out like he was protecting a passenger in his car from an impending crash. Had I not been so emotional, I would have thought it was a sweet gesture that he felt the need to protect my mom from whoever was bursting into the room.

My teeth were pressed together as I sucked in a breath, not even sure where to start.

"Oh! Are you here to read too? Good, good, come sit then." Mom found her spot on the bed and patted the open spot next to her. "We were just getting to the good part, weren't we?" Mom asked.

Jackson's eyes never left mine. "We were very close to the good part, yes."

Blood rushed to my cheeks. Adrenaline I had built up on the ride over had no outlet. Mom was calm and happy, just like the nurse told me on the phone. Anything I was about to say or do would only upset her. I kept my eyes locked on Jackson's, slowly inching to the rocking chair. "Please...don't let me interrupt. I just wanted to hear the story, I can't wait to know the ending."

Mom smiled. "Oh! We're reading a story? I love stories." She looked at Jackson, glancing at the book they had been reading as if the story was just beginning. "Go ahead, Dylan, let's read the rest then."

The name confusion broke Jackson's gaze, my silence giving him permission to keep reading. He looked at her, smiled, and buried his head in the book he had been reading out loud. "The puppy followed his nose down the grassy hill, home at last. 'Look! said Sally. There's Buddy! He's home!'"

"Oh, the puppy is home, that's good, that's very good..." Mom said, patting Jackson's hand as he turned the page.

When the book ended, I kissed mom on the back of her hand and thanked her for a great time, telling her I had to show Jackson to his car.

"Oh, I do enjoy visitors, so lovely," Mom said.

"I know," Jackson said. "I enjoy them too. I'll see you—" he paused, looking in my direction. "I um, am not sure when I'll be back. I'll have to check my calendar."

"No rush, dear. I have a Christmas dinner to shop for this weekend anyway, you take your time. Keep the garage door open for Roger on your way out, he should be home soon, mmmk?"

"What the hell do you think you're doing here?" I hissed, crossing the parking lot and storming as far away from the building as I could.

Jackson quickened his pace to keep up but said nothing, letting his sneakers scuff on the pavement like a teenager who had been caught sneaking out.

"It's not what you think," Jackson said.

"You have no idea what I'm thinking," I said, turning around to face him once I reached my car. Even though it was a cooler night than usual, I pulled off my sweatshirt, thinking about Mom's comment about it being Christmas. "She thinks it's Christmas next week and we're at the end of July. In what reality is this fair to her or me that you start coming around here to keep yourself in my life?"

"This isn't *about you* Pippa, not everything is!"

"Then what is this? I don't understand."

"No, you don't understand. It won't happen again, don't worry." Jackson started to walk away and my voice cracked as I called after him.

"Sure, walk away, *again*. That's what you're good at right? Getting involved and then walking away!"

Jackson spun around, his face nose to nose with mine so suddenly I wasn't sure I even blinked before it happened. "You don't understand, Pippa! I'm not here for you or for *her*," he said, pointing to the nursing home. "I'm here for *me*." He stood frozen with his hand in the air, not able to get the next sentence out. "Why does everything have to be so encrypted? Why can't we just...*be*."

I opened my mouth but nothing came out. "I...I don't know," I said finally.

"I'm part of a volunteer group that Palmetto hospital referred me to. It's for veterans and we read to patients who have Alzheimer's. We get just as much out of it as they do. I had no idea she was your mom when I first started here months ago, not at first anyway."

I almost cut him off to tell him I was aware of the program. I was the one who designed it, having it incorporated in my department's discharge procedures, but I realized he still didn't know how we first met.

"What do you get out of it?" I asked.

"It's nice to be understood."

"She doesn't even know who you are, Jackson. She called you Dylan."

"It doesn't matter what she knows or doesn't know." He brushed an imaginary piece of lint from his shirt and looked away. "It's nice to spend time with someone who understands what it's like to not remember things. Reading is supposed to help with my memory loss issues since it's a type of brain stimulation therapy. She's not going to judge me anymore than I would judge her."

I looked away, embarrassed I had been so angry at him. "Jackson..."

"I've been doing this since before I met you. I didn't know she was your mom, I swear it. She showed me some old pictures of her sister one day and that's when I knew. You two could have been identical twins. I didn't know you and your mom had different last names."

I sighed. "Yeah, she wanted me to have Roger's last name, just in case he decided to come back from Cambodia and we became a family somehow."

"It's funny, for a while after that day we raced on the beach I thought you looked familiar. Something about your face...I couldn't put my finger on it. I guess I just saw a bit of resemblance between you and your mom before I made the connection, so it made sense then."

I was suddenly thankful we were surrounded by darkness because the guilt I felt with his confusion pushed me harder into my car door as I tried to distance myself from him.

I was an awful person.

"So why keep coming back here then once you knew she was my mom? Why didn't you just tell me?" I asked. "Especially after our fight..."

"They told me how much my visits meant to her, how happy they made her. I couldn't take that from her no matter what was going on between us, that wouldn't be fair to her."

I bit my bottom lip and closed my eyes. "Thanks for that," I said.

I meant it.

He nodded. "I didn't tell you because there's things about me that *I* wasn't ready to acknowledge. They're things I'm trying to work on and this program is helping me do that but it doesn't make it any less embarrassing."

He's finally opening up to me...

"There's nothing to be embarrassed about, it's a great program. She called you Dylan," I said, half smiling and trying to lighten the mood.

"I'm okay with that," Jackson said, inching closer.

I crossed my arms in front of my chest, leaning back on the car. Jackson moved to position himself right in front of me, arms at his sides, standing so close that I could feel his fingertips brush the fabric of my jeans and it made my next inhale sharp and shallow.

"I don't mind being put on the back burner, just don't leave me there." His voice was smoother than the night sky.

As I looked up the only thing I could focus on was his lips.

"Come with me, I want to show you something," he said.

"Huh? Where?" I said, breaking from the moment.

"There's something I need to show you. It's important."

I hesitated as he stepped away, opening his palm and motioning for me to take his hand. Realizing I was guarded still, he set his arm down and rubbed his fingers together. "Follow me in your car then, please? It'll only take a few minutes."

I nodded, pangs of guilt guiding my decision. I felt bad for second guessing his involvement with the volunteer program and his intentions.

We drove to the midway point between the nursing home and my apartment, pulling into a parking lot with a strip of condos lined up right on the coast.

I cautiously exited my car, Jackson's face beaming. "What do you think?" he asked making his way up the sidewalk to the one building.

"What do I think about what?"

"Come see the inside," Jackson said, pulling a key from his pocket then shaking his head, laughing to himself as he punched a code into the keypad attached to the door. "Still getting used to this dumb thing."

"Jackson, I don't think I should—"

His eyes met mine. "I'm only expecting you to stay for five minutes. Promise." He crossed a finger over his heart. The smile he was trying to extinguish couldn't let me walk away, so I texted Meg I'd be later than I originally told her and headed inside behind Jackson.

The apartment was completely bare with the exception of a futon in the living room. The kitchen was fully stocked and had an impressive open floor plan that I envied. "Nice place," I said, peering down the hallway. "So this is where you wound up, huh?"

"Okay this is the best part, look here," he said, power walking down the hallway toward one end of the apartment.

"Jackson," I said, peering down the hallway. "I don't know what you think is going to happen here but..."

"Just *look*," Jackson pleaded, pushing a door open and pointing inside.

I hesitated, watching him bounce between happiness and nervousness.

He said nothing and cocked his head to the side, motioning me to look inside.

I exhaled, moving toward the door.

Peering inside I took note of the four walls, and the oversized floor to ceiling window that I'm sure overlooked the ocean when it was daylight out that would let in an impressive amount of natural light. Two built-in bookcases lined the back wall, and two full-sized hinged doors undoubtedly opened up to reveal a double length closet.

"It's a bedroom, all right," I said blankly.

"Isn't it perfect?"

"I'm happy for you," I mumbled turning my shoulder to head back down the hallway.

That's when I felt Jackson's hand on my shoulder. "This bedroom is for Phoenix," Jackson said. "There's two more bedrooms just like this one."

My heart stopped. "What did you say?"

"Well, you never let me come to your place but I knew you didn't have two bedrooms from what you told me. I had to assume on the days or weekends you had Phoenix it was probably a little cramped and that's not an ideal arraignment for too long, right?"

I started to back down the hallway toward the front door. "Jackson, I don't know where this is going but..."

"The location I thought was perfect, I figured you'd probably want to be a bit closer to your mom but wanted to stay in the same school district you were in before just in case that was important to you. Is that important to you? This apartment complex is right on the line so you're good."

"We're not moving in with you," I said. "I don't know how you go from leaving me stranded on the beach to thinking that I would forget all of that and move in with you because of a fancy apartment—"

"With me?" Jackson said, shaking his head. "Pippa, no. This isn't *my* apartment." He moved toward me, grabbing my right hand and placing a key inside. "This is an emergency key, just in case the keypad stops working. It's not my apartment, Pippa. I didn't get it for us. I got it for you and Phoenix."

I was shocked. "What? Why? Why would you do that, after everything you said?"

"Everything I said?"

"You told me that it didn't *matter* that I had a daughter with Dylan, that you had nothing to say about it...and then you walked away. You walked away, Jackson! So then you disappear for almost a month and pop up out of nowhere with a surprise luxury apartment? Who does that?"

"It *didn't* matter," Jackson said, lowering his voice and moving a piece of hair from my face. " Don't you understand? I didn't care about the story behind you raising a little girl. I just knew you had one, but it didn't matter, it wouldn't change how I felt about you, Pip."

"Then you left."

"Then I left," Jackson agreed, his eyes pulling me in.

"You left me there," I said, my voice betraying me as I struggled to keep my guard up.

"I left you," repeated Jackson. "Because you were right. I left to work on myself, Pippa. You shouldn't be with me knowing how unbalanced I could be...not unless I did all I could to help myself. I cancelled my lease and moved into a Valor House, it's a residential program for veterans. They're the same place that runs the volunteer program for your mom's nursing home. They help with guys like me, with post-traumatic stress disorder, and I needed to completely immerse myself in it. There was no way I could stand on that beach even one second longer. I had to leave you, right then and there, so I could start fighting for you. I'm fighting for you harder than I've ever fought for anyone in my life."

His hands were now cupping my cheeks. The feeling of his skin against mine was familiar and welcomed. "If you wanted us in your lives so badly why didn't you text or call me? Why did you just disappear?"

" This wasn't just about me. I had to give you time to figure out what you wanted and who you were, too. I couldn't figure things out for you. You needed to know you were stronger than you thought you were." He caressed the side of my head with his thumb. I could feel his palms on the sides of my head then, pulling me close to plant a kiss on my forehead. " I needed time to figure myself out too, that's why I am staying at Valor House. I don't care how long it took, but this apartment is just for me to know that you're both safe and taken care of."

"Jackson, I can't accept this." I looked around incredulously. Jackson was finally letting me into his world. He was kind, and it wasn't as dark as I imagined it would be.

"You can. It's paid up for the year. I planned to stay at Valor House as long as they'll have me. I realized my actions will speak louder than my words ever will. I didn't want to tell you what you meant to me, I had to show you."

"You're sure about this? You're not lying? When were you planning on telling me all of this or showing me this apartment if I hadn't found out you were volunteering with my mom?"

"I'd have no reason to, Pip. I was going to tell you when and if you reached out to me and stopped letting those three gray dots dance on my phone. If you don't believe me you could always ask Meg if you wanted, I called her almost every day to ask how you were doing."

"She knew?!"

"Don't be mad at her," Jackson said, half-smiling at my reaction. "She knew what was going on the whole time but she was a good friend and wanted you to figure things out on your own without telling you what *I* was doing to influence you."

"What do you want...?"

"You, Pippa. Before and always."

He lowered his lips to mine and my knees collapsed into his as I moved with the rhythm of our kiss. His hands slid up the back of my head and he tugged gently, pushing on my lower back to bring me closer to his chest.

"I can't," I said, pulling away and brushing the hair from my face. "I have to go, this is... I don't know what this is but I need to talk to Meg. Now. We're having a sleepover." I needed time to process everything.

Jackson sighed. "I figured that. If your words are going a mile a minute I can only imagine what's going on inside your head. I know it's alot."

"So you can get me this beautiful three bedroom apartment and we live happily ever after then? Is that how it all worked out in your head?"

"Not at all," Jackson said, straight faced. "I think I'm doing all I can to show you that I wouldn't let ex-boyfriends, daughters, or crazy best friends influence how I feel about you. If it means living at Valor House and doing something a little crazy like getting you this apartment for things to start working between us then yeah, I'd do it all again in a heartbeat.

"I don't know what to say," I said honestly. It was an unfamiliar feeling that crept over me, knowing someone wanted to take care of me so passionately. "You have to understand that this feels—"

"It's not too much," he said, finishing my thought. "You're never too much, and if anyone ever tells you otherwise then they're not good enough for you. If in the end we'd still be standing here like this then I'd make the same choices that brought us here in this moment over and over again." He brushed the top of my head with his lips. "Assuming I'll give up on us is like telling the sun not to rise when the moon starts setting. We're both steadfast and a bit impulsive when it comes to the people we care about, huh?"

I nodded, absorbing what he said.

"I'm sure you're dying to talk to Meg now, though," he said, kissing my forehead one last time. "Let's lock up and you can head out."

Chapter 16

"**M**EGAN DESIREE PETERS!" I yelled.

I pushed open her front door, ready to throw a bottle of wine at her head. "Jackson told me everything!" I said, annoyed that I had to stop for a moment to kick off my shoes. I didn't want her to have a head start at finding a place to hide. "I am your *best friend* and you hid this from me? The apartment? His phone calls? Who *are you* even?"

The living room light was on, the TV muted to the weather channel as per every night Meg cooked dinner. I charged into the kitchen. "If you think for one second I'm going to let you not explain to me, in every agonizing detail, the contents of your conversations..."

I walked into an empty kitchen. A full pizza box was on the counter and our usual bottles of wine , waiting for our slumber party to begin.

"Ohhhh okay so we're hiding, great. I'll just yell loud enough for your old lady neighbor to hear and she'll have to call the cops then BECAUSE WE HAVE SOME SERIOUS FRIEND CODES VIOLATED HERE!"

Meg was a child at heart. I walked down the hallway, knowing she was likely crouched down in her office or bedroom, waiting for me to walk in so she could scare the shit out of me. I clicked the light on in her bedroom and glanced around. "You literally have the same size apartment as me plus an office space, Meg. You know I'm going to find you in the next twenty seconds and kick your ass."

Her office was empty too, and my cheeks flushed wondering if I had been yelling to myself the whole time because she ran out to grab more wine or appetizers for when we got the drunk munchies later on.

"Okay then, good talk," I whispered to myself.

As I left her office I heard a faint tapping at the front door. "Ohhhh I would tackle her if she wasn't carrying things," I said, running to the front door and pulling it open. "YOU HAVE SOME SERIOUS EXPLAINING TO—" I gasped, covering my own mouth so I would stop shouting. "Oh, Mrs. Jameson, I'm so sorry I thought you were Meg!"

"Interesting way to greet a friend then," she said, peering inside. "I'm assuming you guys have been fighting all night based on all the commotion?"

"Not yet," I murmured. "I just got here."

"Lover's quarrel?"

"In a way," I replied tactfully. "If there's nothing else you wanted to ask?" I said, beginning to close the door.

"That's all, wanted to make sure everything was okay. Tell Meg that if she's to keep the dog she brought home today she needs to tell the landlord about it or someone else will," she sang.

"A dog?"

"Now dear, I may be old and partially deaf but I know what a full grown dog sounds like from above me. I've lived in small apartments all my life and if it's going to be thudding around all hours someone might complain, that's all I'm saying."

I closed the front door as she walked away. "Meg's allergic to animals," I whispered to myself, peering around. I checked the bedroom and office for a dog cage and when I didn't see one I unlocked my phone to call her as I made my way into the bathroom. "You can run but you can't hide," I said as it rang.

I slipped and was on my back immediately after walking through the doorway. My phone flew to the other side of the bathroom, and I could hear Meg's ringtone echoing off the walls as my head throbbed. Bringing my hand to my face through the dizziness, I screamed at the blood that was pouring down my sleeve.

I grabbed my elbow, frantically using my fingers to search for a gash. I felt nothing, but the blood I was lying in started to soak through the back of my shirt. I forced myself up on to my elbows to get a better look at what happened. I had to figure out where I was bleeding.

That's when I saw Meg.

The razor blade was at her left side. A slit the length of a post-it-note, traveling from her inner right wrist toward her elbow, was pooling blood around her. She was mouthing something, but the room began to spin and I couldn't make out what she was saying. Her back was pressed against the vanity and she was slumped over like a ragdoll, her cheek pressed against the floor. Hollow eyes looked through me.

"Meg," I said, half-whispering.

I shuffled over to her, afraid to stand up with the dizziness. My phone was lying an arm's length from Meg's foot, abandoned. Suddenly weighing as much as a kettle bell, I picked it up. Trying to connect the pieces of gore soaked pandemonium surrounding me, I vaguely remember pressing 9-1-1.

"Nine-one-one what's your emergency?"

"Sixty-two Orchard Lane, she's bleeding heavily and I need an ambulance—I need help!"

I put the phone on speaker and left it on the floor, moving inches from Meg's face, our cheeks practically floating in the blood around us.

"Meg!" I said again, grabbing her face, my own tears unknowingly adding to the mess around us.

Her voice was so soft I had to strain to hear her. "You're early. You're here too early."

My eyes widened. "You're going to be okay, Meg. They're coming. They're going to help you." The operator was growing impatient on the phone in the background as I ignored her statements to remain calm and answer more questions.

"They couldn't help her," Meg whispered, closing her eyes.

"You stay here! Open your eyes and stay here, damn it. Open them!"

A slit of white looked out at me. "Pip, it's my fault. Cheryl."

"Oh Meg, no." I looked around the bathroom, trying to look for an intruder or anything that would explain the slice down her wrists other than a suicide attempt. "You can't leave, you did everything for her. *Everything*." I reached above our heads and grabbed a towel that was dangling. It fell over our faces and I propped myself up on one elbow, wrapping the towel as hard as I could around her wrist as she faded again. I lay back on the ground again, face-to-face with her, and rested her wrist across my temple to keep it elevated.

"Cheryl," Meg said.

"You did all you could. You couldn't save her. No one could. Please don't leave me, I need you. Phoenix needs you. You can't leave."

Meg's eyes fluttered and she mouthed something I couldn't make out.

"You don't have a dog," I said through tears. I had to keep her alert. "Crazy Mrs. Jameson thought you had a dog because she heard a commotion up here but that was just you, wasn't it?"

Meg said nothing.

"I know you blame yourself for Cheryl, I know," I said, lightly petting her head with a blood soaked hand. "You can't do that. You're not responsible for her choices anymore Meg, you have to know that."

"It hurts," Meg said.

"I know," I said. "Help is coming."

"No, it hurts," Meg said again. "My heart...it hurts."

Tears blinded me. The reality of the chaos surrounding us choked me, until I heard the familiar sound of Meg's ringtone going off again. I grabbed at her pockets, not entirely sure how I knew it would be Jackson on the other end.

"Jackson!" I cried into the receiver, losing all self-control hearing his voice. "It's Meg...please help us!" I was sobbing so uncontrollably at that part that I lost my grip on her phone, watching it slide from my hand and bounce away on the floor. My inability to reach it and give him more details without putting Meg's arm down caused him to start screaming into the other end. All he could hear were my cries. I hugged Meg with one arm, pulling her closer to me and burying my face in her hair.

The smell of blood gagged me. My ears started to hum, a high-pitched squeal taking over, a sound I had become all too familiar with when I had anxiety attacks. My breaths deviated from Meg's long and shallow ones.

I didn't hear the bangs on the front door.

I didn't notice the paramedic prying my hands away from my best friend's limp body.

I can't recall the name of the paramedic who wrapped me in a towel and led me outside.

I remember Jackson's face, his legs thrusting him full torque to the ambulance I was sitting in, his car door wide open. He was ghost-white, staring, and rushing into the unknown...something he had done so many times before.

Chapter 17

"I was calling to make sure you were okay," Jackson said, rubbing opposite thumbs together. He was leaned forward in a hospital chair next to Meg's bed. "I was calling to make sure *you* were okay," Jackson repeated. Rubbing his fingertips over his mouth.

"You couldn't have known, no one did," I said.

They had her on oxygen since they had to intubate her when she was brought in but they removed the tube late that morning. The nurse suggested all of her family and friends visit in case things went south. She had lost twenty-eight percent blood volume by the time she was admitted. I had spent a few hours in a bed myself when they first brought us in, coming down from a panic attack. A combination of blood and adrenaline set me off somehow.

Dylan switched on and off with me visiting at the hospital, keeping Phoenix far away. We agreed we only wanted her to remember Aunt Meg in the way she should be remembered: alive.

"Meg isn't the kind of person to tell people when she's feeling down, not outwardly," I responded.

"I know, that's what makes it so much harder. Why do you think she did this?"

"Cheryl," I said sadly.

"She blames herself? She died of a drug overdose didn't she? She couldn't have prevented that."

"She felt responsible. Cheryl asked for help for months from the VA doctors. She was admitted twice in two months for failed overdose attempts. They sent her home from the hospital when she outright told them she didn't feel ready to go home."

"Meg heard her tell them that?"

I nodded. "She was there to pick her up, they said they had no other choice but to send Cheryl home since they held her for the maximum time they were required to. Short of walking outside and shooting up again, there was nothing else they could do."

"So what did she do?"

"She went home and shot up again. That time, she didn't come back."

We listened to the monitors buzzing around Meg for a few moments in total silence.

"PTSD," Jackson said, finally.

I nodded. "Cheryl saw things I don't think most people could ever prepare themselves to see. She was in situations fresh out of high school that even seasoned veterans would want to erase from their memories. She did the best she could when she got back, but something was just..."

"Different," Jackson said, finishing my sentence.

"She got lost, and she just couldn't find her way back."

Jackson nodded, exhaling. "I know that feeling."

"Then you'll understand why Meg feels responsible. She felt like she had to be Cheryl's voice. She feels she didn't fight hard enough for her to get treatment. Meg saw what VA services they provided her and it was nowhere near enough to what she actually needed to get better. She fought hard for her. She made calls, got referrals, took her to doctor appointments and meetings. She complained to anyone and everyone who would listen about how poorly they were treating her addiction. The system seems so broken."

"Is that why you spent time with me? 'Cause you knew I was in the military and you wanted to make sure I got the services I needed if I needed them?"

The question caught me off guard, especially considering he had no idea how bad I knew it could get. The tone in Jackson's voice made the hairs on my arms stand up.

"No, Jackson. That's not why I wanted to spend time with you."

"Then why?"

I moved closer, taking his hand into mine and caressing the top. "I think you know why...don't you?"

Meg groaned, turning her head to the side and we both looked up, expecting her to open her eyes. We held our breath, watching the rhythm of her chest fall and rise under the blankets.

"I consider her the first friend I made when I moved into town, did you know that?" he said

"I didn't," I admitted. "Meg didn't seem to know you well at all, the day she tried to hook us up, actually."

"Well, we weren't really *friends* then. It's not like we grabbed burgers and checked out the pier together or anything, but she listened. I would sit at local bars for hours. It was hard to find a bar on the east side that wasn't packed full of people but at The Inlet I could sit and think for a while without being bothered."

"Meg let you sit and think?"

"Not for long," Jackson said, laughing. "She wouldn't shut up once she knew I was receptive to small talk every once and a while. There was always a guy or customer to complain about. The damn salt wasn't white enough for her one time, I swear it."

I laughed, remembering the first night Meg and I met and how we became instant friends. Our bubbly personalities and inability to shut our mouths once alcohol was involved fused a bond no sword could break.

"Meg and I only really became friends after she tried to set us up on a blind date that day. I had only gone to The Inlet a few times before that, maybe once or twice after I started working the volunteer program. Some other bartender was there back then. Sydney? Sue?"

"Yeah, Susan," I replied. "She's the owner but you usually only see her there for lunch hours now. She hired Meg to get more of a break."

"That's right," Jackson said, wagging his finger at me and leaning back in his chair to tuck his hands behind his head. His lips peeled back to expose a handsome row of teeth and his nose crinkled just around the edges.

He's gorgeous, Meg wasn't wrong.

"You okay?" Jackson said.

"Yep, totally fine. I'm—I was just thinking..."

"I gave a vial of sand to a stranger there once. I didn't even know them."

"You did what?"

"Yeah I know it sounds dumb. I used to carry around a vial full of sand from my time in Iraq," Jackson said, giving me the first real glimpse into his past as a Marine. "It helped ground me sometimes, to reach into my pocket and feel it there. It reminded me it was real, that I didn't imagine everything I'm trying so hard to forget. I was sitting at The Inlet one day, just about a week before we met. I had been working the volunteer program at the nursing home for a few weeks at that point. Your mom was the one who taught me to stop holding onto the parts of my past that didn't make me a better person. She also told me to do one good deed a day, she asked me almost every time I visited. So, one day I gave your mom the vial of sand from Iraq. It made her so happy, it lit up her face in a way I've never seen before. From that day on I started giving vials of sand to people who, I thought, needed some happiness. I'd take the sand right from the beaches here and fill them. I saw a woman having lunch with a friend at The Inlet one day and I asked Susan to put it on her tray of food before she brought it over. I finally let Iraq go, and it felt so good that I wanted to do it over and over again."

My eyes widened. "Jackson that is the sweetest thing that—wait... you *lied* to me. You knew who I was the day we met racing on the beach, then."

"What? No, I didn't."

"Jackson, you gave *me* that vial of sand. I was sitting there having lunch with Meg when Susan brought our food over so you must have recognized me fr—" I clasped my hands over my mouth, literally preventing myself from speaking anything more.

"No, it wasn't you. I gave the vial to Susan and pointed to a woman who I thought looked sad but it wasn't you, it was..." He trailed off, looking into my eyes as if they would reveal the answers I was trying to bury. "It...it was...*it was...you*, wasn't it?"

"Jackson..." I started.

He nodded slowly, the pieces falling together in his head. "Why were you about to say that I must have recognized you at The Inlet that day? I just figured you looked familiar to me because of the pictures you mom showed me, but now..."

His eyes searched my face, looking at the hands still frozen over my mouth. I could feel a bead of sweat trickle between my breasts as everything I had tried so desperately to keep from him started to unravel.

"Let me explain, Jackson..." I whispered, pulling my hands away from my mouth and clasping them together in front of me. I had unintentionally jogged his memory by telling him I was at The Inlet that day and that he must have recognized me. I watched the connections ignite in his eyes.

It seemed like hours before I saw Jackson blink. His forehead had a way of producing a single deep crevice horizontally across his face when he was deep in thought. That moment was no exception. "The hospital," he said at last. "It was *you* at the hospital, the nurse who helped me. It wasn't a dream."

Meg's monitors exploded with an orchestra of noise the moment Jackson spoke, and they scared me just as much as they excited me.

Meg could hear us, she was waking up.

"Jackson," I said, keeping my eyes on Meg.

"You were in my room," he said with widened eyes. "You were there. You saw me when I was...when I was..." He opened his palms to exemplify the emptiness he must have been feeling.

"I was going to tell you," I said.

"When?!"

"I don't... I didn't have a specific time in mind."

"So you weren't going to tell me at all. You were going to pretend that we met racing on the beach? Was that going to be our story? When friends would ask at future dinner parties or when we grew old together and our grandkids wanted us to retell the story of the day we met which one were you planning on telling? How you took care of me in the psych ward or how we tried to beat each other in a race on the beach?"

"I deserve every bit of anger you're feeling right now, but for Meg's sake let's keep it down so she—"

"Ugh, is that why you kept me around!? Was I some kind of charity case or project for you? Did you get extra credit from your boss for treating me outside of work? Was it a bonus if we slept together?"

"No, Jackson! It was complicated—"

"It's not complicated at all! You say 'Jackson, we actually do know each other. We didn't meet racing on the beach, I was one of your nurses and I let you fall for me because I felt bad for you.' It must have been exhilarating to see if your hard work paid off as you followed up on me. All this time I was just an intriguing patient you wanted to check up on."

"That is *NOT* what happened Jackson and you know it!"

"Now who's being too loud?" he shouted at me.

I opened my mouth then looked at Meg. I sat back in my chair, smoothing my sweatshirt. "You're right, Jackson. I know I should have told you sooner."

"Me putting that vial on your tray before Susan brought it out to you was just fate. Then I met you, and everything in my life felt lighter somehow. You were inadvertently the one who gave me the idea to keep bringing vials of sand to your mom, don't you remember that? You said you wished there was a way you could bring the beach to her, so after I gave her my one from Iraq and, after I knew who she was, I kept bringing them. *She* was the one encouraging me to keep doing it, to keep giving people something to feel happy about."

I swallowed hard, feeling like we were ending a relationship I was never a part of. "I knew it was you when we raced on the beach that day," I admitted. "You didn't remember me, though, so I didn't want to scare or embarrass you. I knew memory lapses were possible from the medications and episodes you had from your PTSD. I didn't know how to bring it up without ruining our chances of getting to know each other."

"That's why you didn't tell me? You didn't know how to tell me you thought I was crazy?"

I could sense a hint of sarcasm in his voice but I didn't want to risk it. "I knew you weren't crazy, Jackson. I had feelings for you when I knew I shouldn't."

Meg's monitors beeped in response. She groaned and lifted her pointer finger on her left hand.

"I think she's waking up," I said, scanning the monitors.

"Are you sure? Should I go get the doctor?"

"Not yet," I said studying the screens some more before returning to our conversation.

"I think I heard enough anyway," Jackson said, pushing his chair against the wall and standing.

"You don't need to," I said, not wanting him to leave.

He put his hands in his pockets and looked at Meg. His fingers lifted the edges of his pocket from the inside, and I wondered how many times a day he searched for the vial of sand he had given my mother before reminding himself he no longer needed it. "Text me when she's awake, okay?"

The door slammed with heaviness only my chest understood in that moment, and I felt pieces of me floating away as I watched him walk down the hall. I craned my neck until I couldn't see him anymore.

"Proud of you, friend. You finally told him," Meg whispered.

I whipped around, smiling and clutching my chest. "Oh Meg, you're awake." I ran to her side and gingerly turned her chin in my direction when she tried to turn away from me.

"I'm an idiot," she said finally.

"I won't disagree with you on that, but we don't have to talk about that right now," I insisted. "I just want to sit here and hold your hand and think about ways to get you back for practically making my heart stop."

"Fair enough."

"In pain?" I asked.

"I've felt worse."

"I know," I said gently.

We sat there holding hands in silence, clenching until our knuckles were white. I looked at the bandage wrapped around her opposite wrist, wondering if her initial plan had been to cut both of them.

"What's worse, losing him just now or losing yourself if you *didn't* say anything?" Meg said finally.

I let the first tear slide down my cheek as I considered her question. We clenched hands harder, and Meg shifted so I could lay in the hospital bed with her. "What's worse for you, losing Cheryl or almost losing yourself last night because you *did* say something?"

Tipping our heads together, both of us let tears fall in silence.

"Meg? You know you did *everything* right. There's not one person you didn't try warning and no lengths you didn't go to. You fought harder for her than anyone should have had to. So can I tell you something?" I said, remembering the advice she had given me at the gym.

"Sure, Pip."

"You need to keep fucking going."

Chapter 18

"I wasn't expecting to see you after our last session, so I'm glad you called," April said, closing the door behind me as I entered her office. She smiled and opened her palm to the room, inviting me to sit down in whatever chair I wanted.

"I know we left on a bad note last time, I'm sorry," I said.

April held up a hand, closing her eyes and shaking her head. "Never apologize for the way you feel about something. It's out of our control, the emotions we have when we're hurting or upset. No apology needed. We just need to work on how they're expressed."

"I'm not sure where to start."

"That's usually the hardest part, so why don't we talk about where *not* to start for this session instead?"

"Sure," I said, plopping down into a purple armchair in the corner. "I think we can stay away from any topics about my mom, considering last time."

"That's fair," April said nodding. "I can respect that. Besides, I think it has been quite a while since we talked about a much more important topic."

"What's that?"

"You."

I nodded. "Also a touchy subject."

"It usually is, for most people. You've only been in here a few times this past year. Once just after you visited your mom when she was lucid—er, I mean—after *that one* visit with that person we're not talking about today, and a handful of times after the bombing."

I winced. The word 'bombing' brought immediate visuals to the forefront of my mind. Panicked people running around screaming, the humming in my ears I couldn't turn off, and the blood. All the blood.

"I've worked at a hospital for such a long time, and things that never bothered me before suddenly do."

"Can you tell me which things?"

I shrugged. "Sometimes little things, like blood or the atmosphere of the emergency room. If a patient is having an episode and screaming or can't settle it makes me anxious, it never used to before. The blood still reminds me of Meg, sometimes."

April nodded, leaning back in her chair, eyes intense. "That's not unusual considering what you've been through. Post-traumatic stress disorder isn't a blanketed diagnosis, it can be triggered by so many different things depending on the person or circumstances."

"What do I do if I'm triggered but working at a hospital then? I work in the mental health unit. I can't just disappear or take a break every time I see something that's triggering, I'd be in the break room most of the day."

"Have you considered a career change, Pippa?"

"Never."

"Because you love what you do?"

"Every day."

"Or do you feel you owe something to Meg, that you have to keep fighting the good fight for veterans and save them to make up for Cheryl? To prove to Meg that you're a good friend by committing your life to the cause because other doctors overlooked her as a veteran who was suffering and only saw a drug addict?"

"That's ridiculous, I don't have to prove anything to Meg she knows how much I love her, she's my best friend," I said, my voice hardening.

"So what advice do you think Meg would give to you about your career, knowing your triggers and loving you like she does...as a best friend?"

I opened my mouth. I closed it when I knew where April was trying to go with the conversation but I wasn't willing to admit it out loud.

"You're allowed to make changes in your own life that benefit you and *only you*, Pippa. You don't need permission from anyone and you don't need to prove your strength every day by continuing to stay somewhere you have to fight so hard. Staying at the hospital— now that we know what your triggers are in chaotic, unpredictable environments—would be like living in a beehive when you're deathly allergic to bee stings. Does that make sense?"

"It's like a constant attack," I said, agreeing. "I get it. I just don't know what else I would do. I worked so hard to be in the department I'm in. They've been wonderful with giving me light duty and time off whenever I needed it, I don't know anywhere else I would be treated so delicately."

April smiled, choosing her words carefully. "You're touching your bad ear again, which tells me you're self conscious about making a big change. Remind me, who was the one who created the volunteer program that goes to your mom's nursing home?"

"I thought we weren't talking about her," I said squinting, trying to figure out her angle.

"We're not, we're talking about the volunteer program through your hospital."

"Okay...I mean technically it was my idea but it's not run by the hospital per say."

"So what if that program expanded? You seem to know how to get things up off the ground and running, you have a passion for working with veterans and there's certainly a need for the services they're giving. Seems like a win-win to me."

"There's not a whole lot of funding for programs like that. The only reason why that one worked is because the hospital was backing it financially and I knew Valor House would be a benefit to our discharged patients who were veterans."

"Mmmmhmmm..." April said.

"So, it's not so simple. I'd have to develop relationships with every hospital and nursing home in the area, collect data on the patients and veterans to prove the program works. Then I'd have to proposition the board at each of the hospitals to allocate funds to build up the program and keep it running, funds for figuring out transportation for veterans who get discharged if they don't have it and running background checks on the volunteers. They'd probably have to have a whole department to cover all the work that would be involved."

"I wonder who could make the decision at *your* hospital to create a dedicated department?"

"Well, that would be Mike for sure. I mean, Henry is technically the program director for those kinds of things but ultimately Mike is the one to get things moving. He's the one who gave me the green light to start the program and get Valor House to work with us by accepting referrals. He's also on the board so it made it easier when it came up to vote on."

"Sounds like you got things pretty figured out then," April said.

"No, I—" I crossed my legs, moving my one leg up and down in frustration. "Yeah, I see what you did there."

"Not a bad idea, huh?"

I stared at my knee as I answered. "I guess it's not too bad of an idea, no. The hospital doesn't run the program though, other than us handing out a pamphlet and referring them to Valor House it was out of our hands, the hospital never even knew what patients followed up with the services."

"See a need fill a need, I guess?" April responded. "Probably wouldn't be hard to get a program running internally for something like that considering all of the good that has come of it so far, no?"

"Maybe."

"You're smiling."

"Am I not allowed to do that while therapy is in session?" I said, teasing.

"I encourage it, very much actually."

"It's a good idea," I said, agreeing. "I'll consider it."

"Good. I knew you would. How is Meg now? She has been home for a few weeks, right?"

"I would say she's good but I had no idea she wasn't good before, until she wasn't. I'd like to think she's getting stronger every day. She's staying busy with work and volunteering at the nursing home to read to patients. She's drinking a lot less which I'm *personally* not a fan of but if it's better for her then..." I shrugged and April laughed at my sarcasm. "I'm drinking a lot less too, so there's that. It's all working out."

"And Jackson?"

I stared, the smile fading from my face.

"What about him, Pippa? What's his story?"

A week after Meg was discharged from the hospital I deleted Jackson's number from my phone. I got tired of watching the three gray dots pop up just to disappear and it was driving making me insane wondering what he thought of me now that he knew the truth about how we really met.

I owed him an apology, a real one, but I also owed him space and the chance to move on from all of the internal heaviness our relationship discovered that we both weren't ready to find.

I looked at the clock above April's desk, thankful that our session was almost over. "I'm not sure," I said. "I think he's still writing it."

Chapter 19

JACKSON
Parris Island, South Carolina

"What's your story, running away from your parents?" said a pimple-faced nobody, who was also fresh out of high school. He had higher cheekbones than the empire state building and his fresh high and tight haircut made it obvious he had man-bun length locks previously. A lighter shade of skin where his scalp resided under his hairline glistened, even in the dim light of the barracks.

I had shaved my head within a few hours of graduating high school. The next morning I woke up and went to the nearest Marine recruitment office, waltzing through the door like I owned the damn place, and put my hands on top of the nearest desk.

"Sign me up for Infantry," I said. "Send me out as soon as you can."

The beefy man behind the desk snickered and chewed on the end of his pen, looking me up and down. "Your parents know you're here?"

"I'm eighteen, I don't need their permission."

"So you're a man now, huh? Did you graduate high school?"

"With honors."

"Any convictions?"

"I have an addiction to sweet tea, if that counts."

"Ah, so you're a smart ass, eh?"

"Sign me up for Infantry," I said again, crossing my arms in front of my chest and stepping away from the desk.

"Do you have any idea what you're getting into here, kid? Have you done any research into the Marine Corps at all? Or are you trying to run away from a broken heart like every other high school graduate who runs in here without their mommy and daddy?"

"There's a girl, yes, but she didn't break my heart. I'm breaking hers by being here to do this. So are you going to give me the paperwork or what?"

"You have a family member killed in 9/11?"

"An uncle, sir. His greatest achievements were being a firefighter and an alcoholic. Never at the same time, of course."

The recruiter looked me over, tapping the pen on the edge of his knee. "I have a better idea. You're too quick-minded to be Infantry. Why don't we discuss some other positions I think your *talents* would be better suited for?"

I smirked. "I think I saw an Army recruitment office a few blocks from here, I'm sure they'll have no problem signing me up for Infantry. Have a great day." I pivoted, heading to the door.

"Take your hand off the doorknob, smartass."

I wiped the smile from my face before turning around. "So you need my I.D. then?"

He hesitated, looking me over one last time trying to figure me out. He motioned with his hand. "Let's see that I.D. then."

The act of signing on the dotted line was easy, along with the testing and physical fitness requirements. After being sworn in, I pushed them to put me on the fastest bus out of town, and a few short weeks later I was riding on the bus to Parris Island with memories of my girlfriend screaming and clawing at my shirt to stay repeating over and over. I didn't regret a thing.

Until they got us off the bus.

I had voluntarily, but unknowingly, signed up to live in a make-shift North Korean prison for thirteen weeks that the United States Marine Corps lovingly called 'boot camp'. Within twelve minutes of being off the bus, I started daydreaming about how my circumstances might be different if I had just taken my girlfriend's hand and ran in the other direction when she told me to.

Two men were crying within the first two hours of getting off the bus, and one more had thrown up on their shoes from anxiety.

We were stripped down, shaved, and had to fill out endless stacks of paperwork. It felt like we marched the length of the island over twenty times, dragging our gear with us from place to place, with our assigned sea bags heavier than the regret of our failure to grasp what we had signed up for.

After a solid forty-eight hours, they finally led us back to the barracks to get a lackluster resemblance of sleep. They were exactly how I pictured them: gray, hot as balls with humidity, and with the smell of fear defecating from the pores of every recruit in there.

"So, did you run away from your parents or what?" asked the pimple-faced guy again. He had thrown his stuff into the locker at the foot of our bunk beds.

I jumped into the lower bunk, putting my hands behind my head, not even bothering to look at him. "My parents are dead, Freddy."

"Oh shit man, sorry. I didn't mean to—wait, my name's not Freddy."

"No shit, it's not? You sure?"

"Yeah man, I think I'd know my own name. What's yours?"

"Not Freddy," I said, jumping into my bed and rolling onto my side. "You sure your name isn't Freddy? Last name Kruger?"

"No, my name isn't—hey!" he called out, instinctively bringing his hand to his face. "You don't have to be a dick about it."

I was on my feet in two seconds, standing inches from his face. A few recruits standing near us stopped what they were doing to watch. "Don't I? I mean, I thought maybe that's exactly the way I need to be about it, and if you plan on making it through this place you better get used to it."

He nodded, watching the crowd form around us in his peripherals. "All right man, no problem here. Everyone was out on the same field today, remember?"

I nodded at him and made eye contact with a few other recruits before settling back onto my bed.

Freddy climbed up into his bunk and tossed around for a while once the lights were out. The faint whimper of crying could be heard somewhere four bunks away but everyone was either too exhausted or scared to call him out on it.

"Nathan," came a whisper above me. "My name is Nathan."

I smirked in the dark, respecting his unabated enthusiasm.

"I'm Jackson."

* * *

I was given the gift of four weeks of solitude, courtesy of the boot camp training protocol. No letters, phone calls, or contact with the outside world meant the freedom to let my angst-ridden temperament spiral wildly out of control.

Between pull ups and drill I was pushing back tears and thoughts of the things left unsaid, not just with my parents but also with my girlfriend, Mackenzie. She had a cluster of plans after graduation that included marriage, kids, and a house somewhere with a blue door. I knew I loved her, but I also knew I couldn't stay in a house where my parents had died, waiting for my life to have meaning again. So I let the Marines take the reigns.

Big mistake.

Week six was the halfway point and the letters from Mackenzie were all that were keeping me going. By week seven, I was practically salivating at the idea of sneaking from the barracks in the middle of the night and running for my life. I planned it out in my head, knowing that if I was chosen for fire watch and was paired up with recruit McKinley I could make a run for it. McKinley always fell asleep, poor bastard, and I would be long gone before he woke up and anyone else noticed. The problem was I was literally on an island, and I had no idea where I would even run. The downright torture they put me through was turning out to be more than I was able to handle.

The pit was the worst.

Smart ass remark? In the pit.

Made Freddy laugh while in formation? In the pit.

Didn't shit fast enough?

Too ugly that day?

Screw up cadence?

Had a weird name?

Blinked wrong?

No pep in your step? Into the pit.

I spent a copious amount of time in the pit.

It was a literal pit of sand that made push-ups impossible and any movement excruciating. Sand would sneak its way into the smallest crevices inside my clothes and make it feel like I was working out while rubbing sandpaper over fresh wounds. Then they would make us lay on our stomachs or backs in the baking South Carolina sun, while the sand fleas had their way with our delicate, civilian skin.

It was their way of teaching us not to flinch under duress. The idea was that if we could learn to let the sand fleas have their way with us, a sniper wouldn't.

I'd have preferred to be shot by a sniper.

It was the last hour of the day, and as per usual Freddy was using rec time to hyperventilate over his inability to remember the schedule.

"So then after that, we go to the mess hall, right?" Freddy said, rubbing some residual sand from his hair.

"We're going to the *chow* hall you moron," Parker chimed in.

161

"Don't call Freddy a moron," I said. "At least he can repel a damn wall without crying."

"I hate heights," Parker replied, kicking the air in Freddy's direction when he snickered.

"It's a mock helicopter, it's not even real. All you have to do is get to the bottom," Freddy teased.

"Shut up, Freddy. That thing is at least a hundred feet in the air. I hate you both."

"I hate you but you still follow me around like a lost puppy," I said.

"That's cause I hate Freddy and he's always around you so I always have someone to pick on."

"Freddy, it's called a chow hall," I said, circling back to the original question. They only call it a mess hall in California," I informed him.

"Oh," Freddy replied.

* * *

"Gentleman, shall we chow?" I whispered as we filed into to grab our food after drill the next day.

"I think we shall," Parker chimed in.

We made our way into the sea of shaved heads and body odor to grab trays. We didn't get much time to eat, but the food wasn't anything to write home about either so the sooner we were done the better.

"You hear about Oswald?" Parker said with a mouthful of green beans. "Bastard went home. What a show he put on when he broke his femur."

"He broke his femur? How did he manage that?" I asked.

"Landed wrong on the course, snapped it straight through the skin. They said a drill instructor fainted but that's not confirmed. You didn't hear that from me and you better not repeat it. Two guys definitely puked though."

"I didn't think if you got hurt they'd just send you home like that," Freddy said.

"I don't think they normally do unless there's a long recovery. I'd imagine he'd need a surgery or two, then physical therapy. It'll be at least a year before he's back in the game. So he gets a pass, and we're here eating this garbage," Parker said, slopping his mystery meat back onto his tray.

I chewed my bread, mulling the Oswald story over and over again in my head. Maybe there would be a way out after all.

The course was a mix of agility, strength, and speed. I felt bad for the guys who clearly looked like they never passed gym class in high school. Even though I excelled in sports and physical fitness regimens I still had trouble keeping up.

I had no idea how I was going to attempt to break my femur, but I decided before I even left the chow hall that I had to try. Mackenzie was waiting for me back home and I had made the mistake of thinking that running away from her would be what I needed to set myself straight. It was an impulsive decision in the mix of my parents dying, high school graduation, and an not knowing where my life was supposed to go from there.

I was an idiot.

Her letters were dwindling, and I was growing impatient with the drill instructors constant harassment.

It was time to go home.

* * *

"Tell me, Walker, are you a god damn moron or were you just born without a brain?"

The haze of what happened started to lift as I regained consciousness, with drill instructors' voices booming through the clouds like a foghorn. "You fell off the wall like a ballerina Walker, it was a true fucking Nutcracker show you just put on. You should get an Olympic medal for stupidity. Can you stand up or—"

I woke up in the BAS hours later. The throbbing in my knee was surreal and it was the pain that finally shook me from my sleep.

"Is it bad?" I asked the physician assistant who walked over.

"You've got a deep bruise," she replied. "I don't think anything is broken, but you might need additional scans to make sure you didn't tear anything."

"How long will I be laid up?"

She looked at a calendar on the wall. "About three or four days until we can figure out exactly what's going on. We already did scans at the ACA, we're just waiting for the results. You should get some rest in the meantime. Best-case scenario? You'll be on light duty for a week or two."

I nodded, laying back on the pillow behind me.

"Mail came," she said, handing me some letters. On top of the mail was a scratchy note from Freddy on one of the envelopes that read:

Sorry you fucked yourself up. At least you don't look like a testicle with teeth on a daily basis, right? (I got that from the movie Deadpool, I don't think I actually look like a testicle with teeth, just trying to make you laugh). Feel better man.

-Freddy

I wondered who he ass-kissed to be able to write the note to me while opening the letter with Mackenzie's familiar handwriting scrawled across the front of the envelope. An address was written across the top left corner I knew all too well—it was only three houses away from my own growing up.

The only time I cried as hard as I did by the end of that letter was when my parents were lowered into the ground. It's the kind of cry that comes from your gut and is oddly satisfying when you're done. I was thankful I was held up at the BAS, because I would have never lived it down otherwise if I were in the barracks. When my sobs subsided to a more human-like level, the physician assistant pulled the curtain back alongside my bed and handed me a box of tissues.

"She break up with you?" she said, her tone all too familiar with the game.

"Yeah, I guess four years is too long to wait around for the person you love," I said.

She nodded and patted my shoulder. "I know it won't make you feel better right now, but maybe she was just the right person at the wrong time." She checked her watch and looked toward the door. "I believe no one else will be coming to holler at us for the rest of the evening. I have a pudding pack in my dinner, do you think you can stomach it? Chocolate always helps."

I nodded, throwing the letter to the floor.

She got up and patted my shoulder again. "There's plenty of time for you, don't you worry."

● ● ●

Ssgt. Murray, my senior drill instructor, was sitting at my bedside when I woke up. He didn't say a word, and it scared the shit out of me when his face was the first thing I saw.

"Senior Drill Instructor?" I said, trying to sit up in bed and wincing in pain.

He held up a hand, motioning me to lie back down. "What's your plan here, Walker."

"Sir...?"

"What's your plan here? Are you going to heal up, get back on the course, and fulfill the potential I see in you or are you going to lie down like a dog in the road and let life roll over you?"

I scanned the room for the physician assistant. When I didn't see her I shifted under the covers to give me time to respond.

"I'm making you uncomfortable, I can see that," Ssgt. Murray said. "You know what else is uncomfortable? Life. Disappointments. Girlfriends who leave you while you're at boot camp."

"Yeah. Uh, I mean yes, how did you—" I looked around for the letter.

"It was on the floor, stained with your tears, princess," he said. When he chucked it onto the bed, I tucked it under my pillow and turned twenty shades of crimson.

"So you got a decision to make here. Do you stay and finish what you started? Or do you go running back to your hometown to be with the girl who couldn't see you through boot camp? 'Cause you didn't need to sacrifice your knee to get out of here, we don't want to keep anyone here who isn't really *here*." He slid his chair back, hoisting his belt as he stood to realign his crisp pants.

"What's the damage, Sir?" I asked as he approached the door.

His hand hovered over the doorknob. "You got a deep bruise, nothing three days worth of rest won't fix. Unless you need another story to go home with, Walker."

I nodded, looking down at my knee then back toward the door. "I guess I'll see you Thursday then," I said.

Sergeant Murray nodded, a slight smirk lifting the left side of his mouth. "Good to hear." He turned the knob on the door. "Oh, and Walker?"

"Yes, Sir?"

"I was never here."

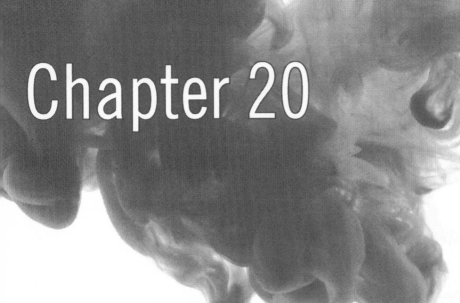

Chapter 20

JACKSON
Iraq

I did a job, no regrets.

It's what I told myself as coalition forces started fighting Iraqi militia in Basra, the second largest city in Iraq. I was in the middle of my second tour, with all intentions of signing up for a third. Maybe even a fourth if they needed me.

I was *salty*, as we called it, a term we used to describe our most seasoned Marines.

I knew things they couldn't teach you, like how the sound of a two-blade helicopter hummed differently than a four-blade. We'd pray for oranges and letters with nudes to open Christmas morning. We'd check our watches on Sundays, hating that it was Sunday, because it meant rice for the millionth time that week.

I hated rice. I tolerated killing people. I loved getting nudes.

The gray areas of whether or not it was justified to kill someone began to blur almost immediately. My fifth mission during my second tour in Iraq was no exception.

The original objective was simple enough: put up a parameter around the city and herd everyone out, picking them off as they channeled out to capture our target.

Master Sergeant Cooper had a better idea.

"This guy we're going after is a monster," I said to Cpl. Freddy, kicking a plume of dust into the air as we sat baking in the sun. I wiped my brow, turning my chin to the sky to determine how much longer we'd have to endure the heat before the sun started to set. "If this is what we have to do to kill him I think we're doing the lesser of two evils."

"Well, you're higher up on the food chain than I am, *Sergeant*," Cpl. Freddy said. "What'd he do that we're gunning for him so hard?"

"Besides the obvious terrorist-daily-agenda items, you mean?" LCpl. Nelson said, rolling his eyes.

I smiled, watching Cpl. Freddy's eyes shift to the ground, something he did when he was embarrassed. It was a miracle we both made it through boot camp together. The odds that we wound up with the same MOS and in the same battalion not for one but *two* tours of Iraq was implausible. Yet, there we were shooting the shit, just after getting word that I'd be heading out that evening on a secret op.

"Hey now, Nelson," I started. "Don't make Moon feel bad. He's not as smart as you and me. As Marines it is our duty to protect and serve even the *dumbest* of human beings. Ain't that right, Moon?"

"My name isn't Moon," Cpl. Freddy said in a monotone.

"Wait, why are you calling him Moon?" LCpl. Nelson asked, a smile spreading across his face in anticipation of the joke before it was even said out loud.

"Look at him," Cpl. Freddy said, pointing at LCpl. Nelson's face and wagging a finger. "He doesn't even know what you're about to say and he's ready to laugh anyway because he's new blood here and thinks this is how you advance your career, by sucking up to cocky sergeants."

"I'm not cocky at all," I replied to Cpl. Freddy. "I just naturally excel at life." I winked at him, turning my attention to LCpl. Nelson.

"And I call him Moon, dear Nelson, because it's nicer than calling him Crater."

LCpl. Nelson doubled over in laughter as Cpl. Freddy shook his head at the ground. "Har-har, Walker, I get it...because moons have craters, right? Like my face?"

"That's right, Corporal Freddy."

"Speaking of, you know some Pfcs are starting to address me as Corporal Freddy now thinking that's my real name?"

"I had no idea," I said. "How rude. They should know better than to make fun of a Corporal."

Cpl. Freddy threw darts at me with his eyes. "Speaking of being lower on the food chain, Nelson make yourself useful for once and grab us some waters."

LCpl. Nelson rubbed under his eyes at he stood up. "Is that an order, Corporal Freddy?"

"Not unless you want to disregard a direct order from your NCO," he shot back sarcastically.

"Anything for you, Corporal."

I watched LCpl. Nelson disappear. "You could have got that water for yourself you entitled prick."

Cpl. Freddy made sure he was out of earshot before speaking. "I wanted to ask about your bum knee before you head out on this mission tonight," he said, his face suddenly serious.

I straightened my back, glancing out of my peripherals to make sure no one had heard him. "Say it a little louder next time man, would ya? The knee is fine. It only gives out after long runs."

"And sometimes when you crouch."

"So I won't crouch."

"Never again? I don't think you have that option here, we spend a good amount of time with our heads down around here."

"It's fine, I promise." I pretended to pick at the dirt living under my nails. "Okay, okay, stop looking at me like that. I'll get it looked at again first thing tomorrow when we're back. Master Sergeant Cooper and I have been planning out this op for weeks, I'm not about to let him down. Tonight is our only shot. Master Sergeant couldn't get approval from the higher ups for this. After tonight this guy's a ghost and we'd rather not herd an entire city when Intel is good on where he is right now. We can get him. You know they suggested I might have to have surgery on my knee and I don't exactly have the time to do that."

"I'm sure sooner than later is best. You've been covering up your knee issues since boot camp. Must be nice to be Master Sergeant Cooper's right hand man. Get it looked at," Cpl. Freddy said, nodding past my shoulder to signal that LCpl. Nelson was on his way toward us.

"At least we don't have to worry about Agent Orange while we're here," LCpl. Nelson said, handing bottled water to each of us.

"What are you talking about?" I said.

"Agent Orange. You aren't familiar? Didn't either of you have family in the military?"

Freddy and I both shook our heads.

Ecstatic that he held some knowledge about the military that neither of us were familiar with he leaned forward on his knees. "Yeah man, my grandpop told me about it from the Vietnam War. It was this herbicide chemical that we sprayed to kill off their crops and food supplies, then used it on the forestry to make bombing targets more visible."

"So what does that have to do with our water?" Cpl. Freddy asked, staring at his bottle.

"They used small quantities of it to defoliate military base perimeters. It absorbed into the soil and water all around the bases, even in the air. Then our guys would have to walk and crawl through the fields they destroyed with the herbicide, exposing them even more."

"I had no idea," I said. "Were there any side effects? How's your grandpop now?"

"Dead," LCpl. Nelson said, wringing out his hands. "Turns out it was pretty nasty stuff. They had some monetary benefits set aside for veterans exposed to it but it wasn't enough. He had a few different forms of cancer. Leukemia and I aren't friends."

"I don't think anyone is friends with cancer," I said. "Sorry to hear about your grandpop."

"Thanks," LCpl. Nelson said. "At least all we have to worry about now is what color smoke grenades we need to set off, right?"

"Red for distress and immediate assistance needed and blue for…" Cpl. Freddy said, trailing off. His stare was blank. I could see LCpl. Nelson look back and forth between our faces, opening his mouth to help guide Cpl. Freddy to the correct answer.

I held up my hand. "We know what it means, Nelson. Shut your trap."

LCpl. Nelson closed his mouth, following my gaze to Cpl. Freddy's face, realizing what was happening. "Oh. OH! Sorry, I know you guys know… I just…"

I shooed him away with a hand. "Go check the wall for nudes. Come back when you have an update."

"Right. Okay, I will."

Cpl. Freddy and I sat in silence, him staring somewhere off in the distance and me staring down at my boots. They were three missions away from needing to be replaced, but they had carried me through afflictions I would never fail to remember. They'd remain on my feet as long as I could, a remembrance of sorts, to keep the people we lost along the way close and in the forefront of my mind. I usually retired them after successful missions with no casualties, only wanting to change them out when things were on the upswing.

"How long was I gone?" Cpl. Freddy asked a few moments later.

"Just a few minutes. I sent the kid away to check the wall," I said, deciding that after that night's mission I'd put in the order for new boots before we packed up camp and moved on to the next area. I looked up at his face, the familiar warmth of his brown eyes reflecting that the moment had passed.

"You up for tonight if I vouch for you?" I asked.

"Yeah," Cpl. Freddy said. "I'm always ready. I just got lost for a minute, you know how it is."

I nodded. "Who do you think was added to the wall today?" I asked, changing the subject.

"Ask the kid," Cpl. Freddy said, smirking as LCpl. Nelson plowed through a group of guys to deliver his update. He screeched to a stop. "You'll never believe who's on the wall this time."

The wall was a sacred mausoleum of love that was lost. It was shameful to leave a Marine when he was deployed, but wives or girlfriends who cheated on their Marine would get special attention on the wall to properly parade the level of dishonor to everyone in the platoon. Their 'Dear John' letters from back home, whether it was them confessing to their infidelity or from another source who was filling the Marine in on what was happening back home, was displayed on the wall. Typically a picture, often their nude ones, would accompany the letter. It was so other Marines would know how to identify and properly avoid them should their paths ever cross with the deplorable ex while in a civilian setting.

It was a cathartic way of dealing with the worst kind of heartache millions of miles away, while simultaneously enlisting the camaraderie of everyone to bear the burden of hurt together—the only people in the world who could possibly understand.

"Sergeant Lopez," LCpl. Nelson gushed, before letting anyone guess.

"Wow," Cpl. Freddy said, shaking his head.

"Yeah, what a shame," I chimed in, already knowing that he was expecting that letter for some time. He had confided in me weeks earlier, so I tried to share in their surprise.

"Master Sergeant Cooper," LCpl. Nelson said, stiffening at attention as he looked over my shoulder.

I stood, pivoting to turn around at the same time. "Master Sergeant."

MSgt. Cooper nodded, putting LCpl. Nelson at ease, while looking at me. "It's almost time."

I nodded. "If it's no bother to you, permission to bring Corporal Freddy with me."

MSgt. Cooper looked around, a dazed look on his face.

"I mean Corporal Sullivan," I said, remembering Freddy's real last name.

"You don't know this Corporal's name yet you want him to tag along on a special op?"

I replied with sublime seriousness. "He has no special skills that I deem necessary for this op, Master Sergeant, however I feel it irresponsible to leave him behind with the rest of the platoon since they'd be subjected to staring at his face."

The cough that MSgt. Cooper let out indicated he was attempting to cover up a smirk and my right cheek twitched with self-evident laughter.

"If you feel his presence would result in a successful mission, Sergeant," he said, nodding his approval.

"I do," I said. "I'd also like to have Lance Corporal Nelson accompany us. He's a little wet behind the ears but the best damn shot I've seen in a while. I'd trust him to shoot the wings off a fly if I ordered him to."

He eyed LCpl. Nelson. "Can you get them caught up, Sergeant?"

"I can."

"He doesn't plan on returning from the op with a DUI like he did while on leave, does he?" MSgt. Cooper replied.

LCpl. Nelson lowered his chin, embarrassed about his recent demotion.

"Master Sergeant Cooper, permission to accompany Sergeant Walker tonight," said a voice from behind us.

We all turned, surprised anyone had been listening, to see Sergeant Lopez standing at ease.

"What the hell for, Sergeant?" MSgt. Cooper asked.

"I've been in the Sandbox long enough to know the best route to take in and out. Lance Corporal Nelson gets lost looking for an MRE most days."

MSgt. Cooper didn't mean to roll his eyes so he shielded his face, dragging the skin on his forehead all the way down to his chin. "Sergeant

Walker has the final say, I trust his judgment more than any of you morons. You leave at 0200 hours. Remember, Sergeant Walker, not a word about this except to your team. I even got one of the operators from the SEAL team to get a squad of four for oversight."

"I think he legit laughed," Cpl. Freddy said to me, watching MSgt. Cooper disappear in the opposite direction.

"Looking for a distraction or something?" I said to Sgt. Lopez.

"Something like that. I made a small contribution to the wall this morning."

"I heard. Is your head in the game? We get one chance at this, otherwise we have to herd the city tomorrow."

"Herd the city?" LCpl. Nelson asked.

"It's when we set up a parameter and leave only one way out, pushing everyone through a small channel and picking people off who look even remotely similar to our guy. If they appear to be a high level threat, children included since they're usually the ones carrying hand grenades to distract us, they're killed too."

"Oh," said LCpl. Nelson, kicking dirt.

"So, it's a little important that we take care of this tonight" I said. "Lopez, why do you want in?"

"I've heard what this guy does. I want to save every woman and child in this city from him. He uses the women to give him children and uses little boys for fun. It's time he comes face to face with some real men."

"Good enough for me," I said. "Okay then, listen up 'cause we have a briefing in twenty with Master Sergeant and you need to have this down..."

● ● ●

The blast from the RPG hit in the opposite direction of where we had entered the building, but it still knocked the wind out of me. Debris littered my chest, compressing my rib cage, and I fought against the ringing in my ears to hold onto consciousness.

The throbbing at the base of my neck told me my head had ricocheted off something.

"Freddy!" I screamed out as the dust began to settle. Listening for sounds of life, I craned my neck and began to push the rubble from my body.

Silence was never welcome in war.

It meant casualties.

Death.

An end to a means.

Sgt. Lopez had been the first through the door. I already knew it meant he didn't survive. The barren floor where he had been standing seconds earlier confirmed that for me. A few scraps of his military uniform, scattered around and doused in crimson, was all that was left.

"Nelson!" I called out, unsure if his keen sense of hearing bestowed him enough time to find cover before we were hit. Pushing myself up onto my elbows I looked around. "Answer me, Nelson!"

The sound of coughing to my right forced me to follow the labored noise through the haze settling around me. Unsure if I should risk calling out again, I whistled.

A familiar whistle returned in response, barely audible but there, and in a pitch I knew all too well.

Freddy was alive.

I knew my legs wouldn't carry me, but I didn't have time to assess my own injuries. Flipping to my stomach I dug my elbows into the ground, pulling my weight across the floor in the direction of the high-pitched melody.

"There's a boulder on my chest," Cpl. Freddy whispered, gasping for air.

I nodded, noting that there was nothing on his chest at all. "Okay buddy, okay, let's see what we can do here." Pain shot up through my legs as I hoisted myself into a high push up, positioning myself to look up and down the length of his body.

A gaping hole where his stomach used to be told me he had seconds left to live. His legs were no longer attached, and the color of his skin matched a fresh winter's snow. I put my hand to my flak, grabbing a smoke grenade. Pulling the pin with my teeth I searched for an area where the smoke would, hopefully, be visible to the SEALs standing by and alert them that there were survivors.

Blue clouds rose from the canister, engulfing the remainder of the hut and escaping through the gaping skylight they had blown into the ceiling moments earlier. A shrill whistle alerted me that the SEALs were close and saw the signal billowing around us.

"It's not so bad, right?" Cpl. Freddy said, eyeing me hopefully.

"Not so bad, ugly," I said, leaning on one elbow and placing my other hand over his chest to feel his breaths and comfort him.

"You're lying. You're my best friend damn it, but you're lying."

"I'm not your best friend, I don't even know why you like me to be honest." I swallowed, scanning the damage around us and knowing he didn't have much time left.

Freddy gasped.

"Don't do that. You're not allowed to say goodbye, we'll get you out of here."

"You're right," he said, shaking his head. "I probably have time to insult you a while longer. You're the biggest jerk I ever knew, you know it?" A tear slid down his right cheek. "I wish I never met you, and you're not as handsome as you think you are."

I smiled. "Your face looks like the spawn of one avocado fucking an even older avocado."

"You know, you always made fun of my acne, but I think it's because you were intimidated by my other features, the ones the ladies prefer," he said, winking through the trembling.

"You're right, man. You'd have made quite the catch. Anyone would've be lucky to have you," I replied.

A thin, straight line appeared between lips where a smile had briefly peeked through. "How'd they know we were coming, Jackson?" Shuddering with fear and adrenaline, his eyes started to drift, but then shot open when he undoubtedly felt the floating sensation that meant he was losing consciousness.

"I don't know, Nathan."

"You used my real name."

"I did."

"It must be pretty bad then."

"It is."

"Jackson?"

"Yeah?"

"You're my best friend...?"

I nodded, letting the tears pool off of my chin. "I'm your best friend, bud."

There was a chance he didn't hear me. He closed his eyes for the last time, taking several shortened and quick-paced breaths before resting soundly in my arms. The canister of blue smoke hissed off in the distance, telling me it was almost empty.

I clenched his shirt, pushing my face into his chest as the SEALs raided the rubble and took hold of me.

"We need to take him," I said, panicked at their rush to drag me out of the hut.

"There's no time, Sergeant," replied one SEAL. "A quarter mile parameter was evacuated, apparently hours ago according to one informant. This whole damn block is a ticking time bomb."

"No man left behind, dammit! He needs to come with us!" I said, struggling to make my way toward Freddy as they pulled at my arms.

"There's no time, we'll come back for the dog tags. Let's GO! Now!"

I couldn't use my legs. They dragged below me, bumping over debris, rocks, and body parts. As we crossed the threshold of what had been the front door, I saw Lance Corporal Nelson curled up in a ball, half of his back blown out by the force of the explosion. He likely died on impact.

"You're the only one, Sergeant," the SEAL said, staring down at my panicked face. "No one else survived. You wouldn't have either if you didn't take cover behind that block wall inside."

"The target?" I asked, changing subjects as I felt vomit rise up in my throat.

"Eliminated in the blast."

Shock set in as we snaked our way through town and it forced my body to convulse with tremors. I fell in and out of consciousness the entire time I was being dragged. Gunfire echoed in the patchwork memories I absorbed on the trip back to base.

When I opened my eyes finally, the soft glow of the rising sun reached into my tent and pooled on the floor, highlighting a pair of combat boots.

"Sergeant Walker," said MSgt. Cooper. "Can you hear me? Do you know what happened?"

I knew he wasn't asking me to inform him that everyone who had accompanied me on the op had died. He knew that already. He needed to provide answers to his higher ups about how a 'simple routine patrol' had resulted in so much carnage.

"Master Sergeant Cooper," I said, nodding from my bed. "You'll excuse me for not standing, I seem to have lost my legs."

"They're still very much attached," he said. "A piece of shrapnel sliced through your right Achilles tendon, so you're correct in being unable to stand...for now. Your left knee is swollen to the size of a basketball, so you likely don't feel anything below the kneecap. It's still there though, Sergeant."

"I don't know what happened."

MSgt. Cooper Cooper shook his head, lowering his voice. "I'd imagine there was a lot that happened very quickly. It wouldn't be the worst thing to not remember. You were close with Corporal Sullivan, is that correct?"

I nodded, Freddy's last words echoing in my mind.

"I'd imagine you have a letter of his he'd want you to send home."

I nodded again, staring at the ceiling of the tent. "Is that all? I'd like to rest if that's okay by you."

"Lance Corporal Nelson, did you know off the top of your head, an address for his wife? I know she's pregnant and I'd like to deliver a message personally."

My face said it all, the reason for his leave a few weeks earlier suddenly becoming clear.

He sighed, half of a smile forcing the corner of his mouth upward. "You didn't know? No, of course you didn't. Smart kid then, he realized you wouldn't let him tag along if you knew."

Water welled up in the corner of my eyes. "I had no idea."

MSgt. Cooper nodded, turning toward the opening of the tent, pausing before exiting. "You know it's lucky the shrapnel only sliced through *one* of your Achilles."

"Master Sergeant?"

"The direction of the flesh wound," he started, drawing a horizontal line across his face in the air. "The clean line it left. I find it *lucky*, that when you positioned yourself behind that block wall inside the building that you took a knee instead of crouching and using both feet to hover. It saved your other Achilles tendon. Maybe even your life."

I swallowed. "Master Sergeant, about my knee. It—"

"Will be completely fine, Sergeant." He lowered his stare. "Your perfectly healthy knee, prior to today, will be fine. We'll take care of you. You understand?"

I nodded.

"Do you feel ill Sergeant Walker? You look paler, I can call the nurse back in."

"It's just a lot to absorb."

He nodded, peering outside of the tent, the sun illuminating crevices of old age around his eyes that had intensified in just a few short months. "It always is. Oh, and Jackson?"

I raised my eyebrows at the mention of my first name, something that was seldom done between ranks, especially when those people weren't particularly close.

"Er, yes, Master Sergeant?"

"This never happened. If you say it did, your time remaining in the Marines and here until we can get you state side will be a living hell. Do you understand? There was no special op, and this was an isolated and unexpected ambush."

179

"Hostiles attacked while on patrol. Understood," I said, nodding.

He raised his eyebrows in my direction, finally exiting the tent.

The weight of survivor's guilt crept into my throat and chest, pushing me under and strangling me with a depth only the ocean could parallel.

Chapter 21

JACKSON
Topsail Island, North Carolina

When they medically discharged me, I chose to relocate to a beach town so I could surround myself by water and be as far away from the memories of the Sandbox as possible. Even though my injuries qualified as an honorable discharge prior to my tour being completed, I wasn't mentally qualified to return back home.

No one is ever *truly* ready to return back to civilian life after war.

I had sold my parents' house the year I graduated from boot camp, auctioning off most of their possessions while states away so I didn't hold onto memorabilia that would weaken my attachment to the military.

After a year and a half of physical therapy, multiple dinners to shake hands with superiors who commended me on my brave heroism while under attack, and visits to the doctors who patched me up when I first came state side, I recoiled into an alternate life amongst locals in a small, sleepy beach town.

The realities of becoming a civilian again hit me in the face like a soccer ball.

"I'd like to get an idea of available job opportunities around here," I said when I got to the counter of the unemployment office, something a fellow wounded warrior told me to do while we passed time talking between hospital beds.

When I signed off on the discharge paperwork I filled out, I was considered seventy-five percent disabled. Injuries from war were on a sliding scale gauge that had no rhyme or reason; a lost limb and hearing loss would make you fifty percent disabled, but PTSD, partial blindness, and a random shoulder pain from lugging equipment around would be considered sixty percent if the person filling out the paperwork asked the right questions. This calculation would be added up, multiplied by some unknown factors, and then spit out to give an estimate of how much the military thought you'd need to be compensated.

The end result? Not much, especially if I ever developed issues down the road from combat, mentally or physically. Disability percentages were calculated at the time of discharge, which was smart on the military's part—they documented problems with exiting military personnel before any long-term effects started to show.

Not that it mattered anyway. It was never about the money, and my parents had left me plenty of it when they passed. I had spent years perfecting my training, learning to be a hardened machine, and a killer when needed. Then they patched me up the best they could, put a bus ticket in my hand, and I was on my own.

The military built us to thrive in an environment where we depended on camaraderie, someone always having your back, and a culture of family that extended outside of your blood born relatives. They never taught us how to survive on our own when we were discharged.

"What kind of skills do you have, hun?" the lady behind the glass wall asked me, shifting papers around on her counter in no apparent order.

"Hand-to-hand combat training, advanced weapons training, survival tactics—I'm sorry, did I say something wrong?"

"I meant what kind of career skills do you have? We can try and narrow down what to look for but I'd need now what kind of *relevant* job skills you're able to bring to the table."

"Well, I just spent one and a half tours in Iraq, so unless you have any jobs calling for a hit man, I guess I'm out of luck." I walked away from the counter before she could respond, thrusting open the doors to the parking lot so violently I thought for a moment I broke one.

They don't teach you how to *not* kill people when you leave the military. There's an awful lot of time spent teaching us tactics to combat, shoot, and take hostile threats down...but they never explained how to undo that training. I was hyped up, taught to be angry at enemies and the injustices that terrorists brought to our country, and then I came back to civilian life and I had no where to put that anger.

So, I kept to myself.

I found odd jobs at construction sites, laboring until the clang of metal or a machine would set me off and I'd have to go looking for a new job. I punched bosses in the face when they tried to control me, brawled with coworkers about their political stances, and stared at the ceiling at night wondering if sleep would ever happen for me again.

Then Pippa happened.

She was stretching on the beach that day, staring into the ocean and looking as lost as I felt.

The race we had was unintentional; I really *was* just trying to burn off steam from losing my job a day earlier. Her spirit was intoxicating, and she challenged me in a way I hadn't felt in so long.

It built slowly, at first, but the more time I spent with her the more I started to feel again. Emotions resurfaced I hadn't felt since Mackenzie; since seeing my parents' faces when I told them I got my acceptance letter to Yale University. I felt euphoria, like how I'm sure Cpl. Freddy felt when he exited the bathroom at that local pub hours before deploying to Iraq the first time, a smile on his face the length of China and a woman exiting shortly after, dabbing the corners of her mouth.

I'm sure it was how LCpl. Nelson felt when he found out he was going to be a father for the first time.

When I found out Pippa was training for the Boston Marathon I knew I had to be a part of it with her. We trained for months, in every element of weather, stealing kisses on the beach and holding hands under the table at Lorenzo's Pizza shop when we carb-loaded.

She was everything I never knew I needed.

She had walls up, I knew. I also knew she had her reasons, like I did. I wasn't going to be stupid enough this time around to let someone amazing walk out of my life without showing her how much she meant to me.

I thought being at the finish line of the Boston Marathon with military dog tags that symbolized a promise to her etched into the back of them would be a moment we would both never forget. I put them in a small blue box that morning, excited to give them to her when she finished.

Pippa wasn't the type of woman who would take my words for truth. She'd need to see how serious I was about her, over time, to get her to finally start taking us seriously and see that we were more than just running buddies. I wanted to spend as much time as I could with her smile right in front of me, and the past behind me.

Then, the explosion happened.

Screams erupted.

I watched Pippa fall to the ground.

I blanked, and when I came to I was at her side, blood in my hands as I held her head. There was a man standing near us and I didn't recognize him. I know I assessed him as some kind of threat to Pippa, I don't know why.

Then, everything went black.

Chapter 22

Meet me at the beach, our spot.

I hovered my thumb above the screen of my phone, barely remembering to breathe. The last time I had seen Jackson was at the hospital with Meg, yet here he was, popping up in my text messages like a memory that refused to fade. I couldn't just leave things the way they were since seeing him last, I had to face him, so I tapped on the screen and hit send before I had a chance to second-guess my decision:

I'll be there in ten.

The second time I witnessed Jackson attempt to kill himself, he was standing at the ocean's edge with a .22 in his right hand.

The early September breeze whipping off the clashing waters, mixed with the darkened skies as the sun began to set, told me that we would be alone for a while. I squinted down the coastline anyway, hoping someone would be flying a kite or walking a dog to witness what was about to happen.

There was no one.

A softer, seaweed-colored haze surrounded his blank pupils. They were a lot like his personality, a mixture of steel and cotton that didn't know how to coexist together.

At that moment the structural frame that kept him together was unfolding.

Jackson's shoulders were hunched as if he were about to get sick—the adrenaline of my showing up to the beach moments before he off'ed himself seemed to shake his confidence in what he had been planning to do.

"You told me when I was hospitalized that this would get easier," he whispered, his eyes locked with mine. He turned his head toward the water, a flicker of air pushing dark strands of hair across his forehead. For a moment I considered grabbing the gun and heaving it as far as I could into the depths of the ocean. I knew better. He would find another way, any way, to end the pounding in his head. He was barely thirty but had a chiseled physique and a fast mile. He'd be head first into the ocean within seconds to find the gun at that point. If he didn't find it, he would simply choose not come up for air.

Right then, I was his air.

"I did say that," I confessed. "This isn't you," I said. I nodded toward the gun. "I know you."

"You don't know anything!"

I flinched as angst forced his trembling hands to rest on the top of his head, the .22 pointed inadvertently in my direction.

In response, I lowered myself to the chilled sand to avoid the barrel of the gun. Patting a spot beside me, I lured him to do the same. His body language told me he would never let me in that easy, but if I could get sand into his hands, I could distract him enough from the agony his face was telling me he felt.

"Do you know what today is?" he asked, wiping his nose on his sleeve and coughing to cover up the pitch in his voice.

"I do," I said, nodding, my eyes widening at the realization that I suddenly knew what had set Jackson off.

"I don't know who I am anymore," he muttered, more to himself. The wind threatened to drown out anything else he said, so I patted the spot next to me with one hand while letting sand drift through my fingers like an hourglass in the other. He watched the crystallized strands flow to the ground, sighing deeply.

That's it, come back to me now.

He crouched, a slight shudder in his left knee, and the next knee followed. The gun came to a rest on his right thigh. Shoulders still hunched, he refused to look at me.

I mistakenly reached out to touch his left thigh and he flinched, looking up and then back down at my hand.

I turned my palm toward him. "Feel the sand with me," I suggested. I was unsure if he could hear the thudding in my chest over the wind.

He stared at me for a moment, then back down at my open hand. Nodding, he rubbed his beard before inching his fingers toward mine.

When our hands interlocked, I put pressure around his fingers and started to bury our hands beneath the cold surface of the sand like a squirrel. Once our hands were mostly covered, we took turns squeezing the sand between each other's fingers in a slow and rhythmic motion.

"You know why I'm doing this?" I asked, knowing that he wouldn't look at me when he answered.

"To bring me back," he replied.

"Yes." I shook my head and we sat in silence a few minutes longer, watching the waves stealthily inch closer.

"Where'd you get the gun, Jackson?"

"It was my dad's" he replied. "Hey, why are *you* crying?" Jackson's voice alerted me to the trickle of tears running down my face that were being supplied by adrenaline.

"I'm okay."

"You're not."

"I don't know either," I confessed.

"Huh?"

"You said earlier that you don't know who you are anymore."

He nodded.

"I don't either," I whispered.

With our hands interlocked beneath the sand, he had no choice but to let the gun slide down his thigh and fall in-between us so that he could cup my chin in his hand. "We've been here before, haven't we?" he asked.

The burn from trying to hold back tears was evident on my face, I was sure. "Yes, Jackson. We've been here before."

"So what happened? Why are we here again? What did we do wrong this time so that we're right back to where we started?"

"It's not anyone's fault. We didn't do anything wrong, we just..."

"We just what?" he asked, his breath lingering on my lips.

I closed my eyes, trying to fight the urge to do what I knew I shouldn't do. "We can't do this."

"We can," he coaxed.

He leaned on his free hand so that our noses were almost touching. The sun had disappeared long ago and the only way we could make out the shapes of each other was courtesy of the stars peeking out from above. "We can do this, we can fix it."

"I don't know if we can..." Shifting my weight, I used my shoulder to gently push against his chest so I could breathe, so I could give myself the space I needed to think clearly.

"Pippa, I love you."

My knee-jerk response to him telling me he loved me for the first time flew out of my mouth. "There's no way you can."

"You have no idea, Pip. I've loved you from the moment I saw you, you have to know that."

"You can't love me," I demanded.

"Why not?" he asked, the desperation in his voice mimicking my own.

"Because you have no idea who I really am," I said. I closed my eyes, not knowing if what I was about to say was going to help or hurt the situation. "I've been lying to you this whole time."

In quantum physics, entangled particles remain forever connected. Actions performed by one impact the other, even when separated by great distances. Entanglement only occurred when particles interacted physically.

I considered the random college lesson lingering in my brain, watching my fingers slide between Jackson's in the sand. It made so much sense now.

"You were thinking of killing yourself, that's why you got me that apartment, wasn't it?" I asked. "That's what you meant when you said you wanted to make sure I was taken care of."

He nodded, his honesty with my blunt inquiry harder to acknowledge than the question itself. "The pain just builds and builds, some days it's just so much. There's nothing I wouldn't do for you, Pippa. I never had a solid plan. Part of me wanted to throw the gun into the ocean before you even got here tonight. I brought it to get rid of it, but I wanted you here with me when I did it. I just couldn't help but wonder if I would need it one day and couldn't bring myself to do it before you got here. I'm sorry if it scared you. I wanted to make sure you were taken care of if I wasn't here, yes, but I decided to get rid of the gun tonight. That's why I texted you. I know we betrayed each other. I made you believe I was worth fixing and you made me believe you didn't know me. But it's like I can feel you from wherever I am, like we're entangled in the same web. All this time I was just hoping you'd just show up one day, ready to go at this full torque with me, however misguided that might be."

"You're not broken, Jackson," I replied. "There's nothing for me to fix."

"I'd take a civilian job anywhere in this world and help raise your girl. I have hollow spots, and it makes me question how you can fill them so effortlessly. I would relive the bad days a thousand times if it meant I could relive all the days I spent with you just once."

"So don't leave me," I said, placing the gun behind me as I said it. I looked out onto the ocean. "Everyone else seems to hold all the right cards in their hands while you and I sit here feeling sorry for ourselves."

"Do we?" he asked. "Feel sorry for ourselves, I mean."

"I'm just sorry," I said.

"So were you going to show up one day and run into my arms like you wanted or was it just a dream you were holding onto?"

I swallowed. "You're the part of my story I never saw coming, the piece that fits and stays no matter how much I try and ignore it, and that scares the hell out of me."

"I've seen scary. I lived it. *This* is not *that*," he said.

"So where do we go from here then?"

He licked his lower lip, focusing on the sounds of the surf. "We stop pretending we don't want to be together."

"I'm not who you think I am," I repeated.

"I know," he said.

"And you're not who you I thought you were."

He nodded. "I know."

"I've been lying to you because I'm *not* the girl made of armor anymore. She's gone and I'm exhausted from trying to pretend she's not. I'm not the fearless girl, or the girl who's going to light up the room with her jokes while I'm feeling so much anxiety..."

"No, but you're my girl," he replied.

Tugging on my hand, he coaxed me to sit in his lap. I shifted my weight onto him, sprawling my legs into the sand to our sides. Both of us glanced at the gun sitting a few feet away, and then he moved my chin so I was facing him instead.

"Today is the day Freddy died, isn't it?" I asked, running my fingers through his hair.

He buried his face into my shoulder, nodding and exhaling in a deliberate attempt to rid his lungs of any air. "I told you that when I was in the hospital?"

"You did."

"What else did I tell you?"

"How about I tell you what I'm thinking instead?" I asked.

His hair rubbed against my shirt in response, and goose bumps prickled my arm as the waves lapped in front of us.

"I'm feeling broken, just like you," I said. "I'm not whole because I've been trying so hard to ignore what I've been feeling."

"What's that?"

"That I love you too, Jackson."

Chapter 23

We agreed to go on a date, a real one.

Trudging through the sand, long after the sun had set and we had thrown the gun into the ocean, we walked back to our cars and planned a date night where we could muddle through all of the baggage and uncertainties from the previous months.

"So did you ever get in touch with Mackenzie when you got home?" I asked between mouthfuls of fries. I was perched on the edge of my couch, surveying the living room and loving how it felt so easy to be in the same room as Jackson.

"I wouldn't do that to her," he replied, muting my TV just as our conversation turned serious. "I wasn't the same person when I came back, and I didn't want her to forget the person I was when I left."

"Did you?"

"Did I what?"

"Want to forget the person you were when you left?"

"That was kind of the point, yes. I wasn't going to be the Yale student my parents wanted me to be. I joined the Marines so I could figure out who I was on my own."

"Do you still think about her?"

"Sometimes."

The idea of Jackson being emotionally attached to another woman vexed me, but I understood it. I didn't think he shouldn't have been having those feelings, but I just couldn't imagine how dismal and dejected his time in the military must have felt. It was a tragedy to love someone but never have the contingency to show them.

"I needed to know who I was first, it couldn't be about her when I first came back."

"And you know who you are now?"

"More than I'd like to some days."

"What do you know?" I asked.

"That I'd still give you the dogs tags on the finish line of the Boston Marathon," he said, resting his hand on my knee.

"What are you talking about?"

"The dog tags I gave you, do you still have them?"

"Maybe," I said, feeling my cheeks abandon the tone I was trying to set in my voice.

"I originally planned to give them to you race day."

"Who wanted to give them to me?" I demanded, remembering how much time and progress he made at Valor House when we didn't speak for a few weeks. "The past or current Jackson?"

"Both. Always."

My mouth hung open, remembering the inscription on the backside of the dog tags he had given me. "Wait, how did you know I was going to ask you that question just now to be able to inscribe dog tags you gave to me weeks ago?"

"I didn't," he admitted. "I guess we just think alike. I wanted you to know that I was going to love you regardless of how you did at the Boston Marathon. I loved you before and I would love you after. The inscriptions just have so much more meaning now."

"What do you mean?"

He took my hands. "I know what it feels like to be trapped inside a body and mind you no longer recognize, when the skin you were born with is not the same as the one you've lived in. If anyone is going to understand what it feels like to have your world turned upside down by chaos and crisis it's me. I had these great expectations of who I thought I would be after the military and I didn't end up being who I thought I would be. I'm not cured, Pippa. There's no *perfecting* the way I try to live my life anymore. I can only manage the cards I'm dealt and make good use of them. Valor House taught me that I don't need to be some unattainable level of perfect before going after what makes me happy. So if you're wondering which version of yourself—past or present—that I love, the answer is still the same. Both. Always."

The heaviness in my chest was crushing. "So what if I told you I wasn't as sure as you that this could work?"

"I'd say, by the way you're touching you ear, you're a bad liar."

"I am not," I protested, moving my hands into my lap.

"But I'd also say that I'm not so sure either."

The words stung. "That's not what I was expecting to hear."

"It's the truth, isn't it? I'm not sure anyone is capable of loving someone they don't know. We don't know really know each other yet, do we? After all, this is our first date."

"Doesn't feel like one," I replied.

"Do you love Dylan?" Jackson asked.

"Technically you're not even supposed to know about him because we haven't brought him up in conversation yet, so I'm not answering that."

"Your non-answer is an answer."

"I will always love Dylan, yes. We have an entangled history no other person can possibly comprehend or judge us for but that doesn't mean I am *in love* with him."

"That's fair."

"It's not fair," I shot back. "My heart feels so big and I want to let you in so badly but I'm so scared. Everyone I have ever loved walked away from me. My mom, Dylan— YOU!" I said throwing my hands in his direction.

"Meg hasn't."

"She tried," I said bitterly.

Silence fell between us. I fumbled the remote then stood up. "Why even ask that question?"

"I asked for a reason, Pippa. I wasn't being a jerk, I just wanted to know if you loved him, because even if you did and you wanted to be with him, who would that be fair to?"

I eyed him. "What do you mean?"

"I had to face who I became when I got home, when I was a civilian again. I was not the same person that I was when I left. Something changed."

"So?"

"So if you think that the bombing didn't change you, that you are still the same person you were before, you're wrong. You're stronger now, more aware. You know what it means to not be invincible. There's power in that, but also a change. I'm not saying you don't love Dylan, I'm just saying... who is that fair to? Probably neither of you. You're setting yourself up for failure by assuming everything about your past relationships would remain the same when *you're* not."

"So what about you then? Why bother trying this with me when we know we both have our things to work out?"

"I'd still marry you right now," he said. There was no hesitation in his words, no indication he thought twice about it.

I sighed. "So what now, Jackson?"

He looked around the apartment, sipping on his beer as he nodded. "I think Meg should move in with you."

"Because you *wouldn't* want to?"

"Because you're good to each other, and you're what each other needs right now. Even if it means you never want to see me again after tonight, I'll be happy knowing that you and I gave it an honest try and that you're living your life surrounded by people who love you."

Chapter 24

"**M**y feet hurt," Meg groaned. She reached for a chair to her right and slid it out, clunking her feet on top and sighing. "Ahhhhh, that's better."

"Real classy to put your feet up at a restaurant," I said, looking around to see if anyone was offended.

"This is a *real* classy place," Meg agreed. "Have I never brought you here before? The Inlet is a local hot spot for celebrities and escargot, everyone knows that."

"Your feet wouldn't hurt so bad if you didn't own so much crap. It really shouldn't have taken us a full two days to move you into my apartment."

"*Our* apartment," Meg corrected. "And I don't have that much stuff, the boxes only take up half the living room. Do you think I need to actually unpack everything or could I live out of cardboard boxes for a while?"

"I've seen stranger things," I admitted.

We melted into our casual Sunday routine like a slow burning candle. A wispy breeze rolled off of the ocean, enveloping us in the aroma of sea salt and seaweed. The Inlet had its usual slow-paced crowd, our spot out on the deck was still the one with the best views, and we both happened to show up wearing practically the same outfit once again but...

Something had changed.

Meg was composed and serene, staring out at the ocean with clear eyes with an aura that beamed through her hooded sweatshirt. Whenever she was deep in thought her fingers would lightly dance over the skin on her wrist that was hidden beneath the long-sleeved shirt.

I felt different, too, and joined her in staring at the ocean. Waves crashed up against the shoreline, pulling the sand and shells back with it. Each time a new wave appeared the sand composition would inevitably change with the rush of water and pull of the undertow.

"He ruined my life," I said, putting my chin in my hand and pouting. "I'll never be able to look at garbage cans sitting out by the curb or read to my mom without thinking of him."

Meg shook her head in disagreement. "Your eyebrow lady can ruin your life faster than any man can, sweetheart."

I snorted. "Do you think people can change, but still be the same?" I asked.

Meg was still staring at the mesmerizing transition of waves to sand. "How so?"

I shrugged. "I mean do you think you can love someone, but something forces them to change who they were—so they're not *really* the same anymore but there's parts of them that are still the same person you fell in love with."

"I think you can learn to love two different versions of a person, Pippa. I don't think love has to be so black and white. If it was, I honestly don't think many people would experience it. There are gray areas and people learn to grow through mistakes or experiences. I thought I loved myself before, but now that I'm in a different place mentally, I don't think I knew what true self-love really was. I still have some learning to do. So I guess the real question floating around in that brain of your is, do you love the difficult, hard to manage pieces of Jackson or just the calm, gorgeous ones?"

"Both. Always," I replied. "But I feel like I'd have to get to know him all over again to know for sure."

Meg nodded, looking past my shoulder. "So go get to know him."

I sucked in a breath and spun around in my chair. Jackson was standing on the deck, his hands clasped in front of him. The breeze ran through his hair like a wild horse, his face telling me he was there to tell me something important.

"Meg, you called him?" I asked.

She nodded, taking a sip of her drink.

"You don't do that," I hissed. "You don't call people from your bar, remember?"

"I think we all have some growing to do, Pippa," Meg said. She slid her chair back and stood up, making her way toward Jackson, but not before lowering her head to my ear. "There's nothing about *either* of you that's unlovable." I watched her walk away, wishing the butterflies in my stomach would fly away with her.

"You're here," Meg said to Jackson.

"I'm here." Jackson kept his eyes locked on me as he answered.

Meg looked back over her shoulder. "I'm going to hang out at the bar, it's a bit too crowded out here for me." She turned back to Jackson. "Thanks for showing up," she said, touching his arm gently as she stepped past him. She paused two feet away from him and turned back around. "Oh, and Jackson? In case I've never told you, thank you for your service."

Jackson closed his eyes. "Welcome home," he responded.

"Huh?" Meg asked, turning around.

"If you want to thank someone for their service in the military, tell them welcome home. We're not always proud of the things we had to see and do while we were away to warrant thanking us. We do our jobs, no regrets, but most of us don't come back the same person. So to welcome us home when it's finally over, regardless of who we are now... that's something."

Meg eyes glanced from the back of Jackson's head to my face. She smiled and nodded. "See, Pip? Always growing." She turned on a heel, calling over her shoulder as she headed toward the bar. "Welcome home, Jackson!"

Pushing my chair back I walked over to him, thankful that the deck was deserted and that the embarrassment of getting caught off guard by his presence wouldn't be witnessed by anyone else.

I opened my mouth but he abruptly held up a hand.

"I'm scared to start over too, because there's a chance the outcome won't be what I want, but I'm more scared to not try and never know. I want to do one thing every day that will make you look at me the way you did that first day on the beach. You're the one person I feel I don't have to hide from, and I need you to know you don't have to hide from me either. I'd like to find out."

"Jackson..." I said inching closer to his chest, letting my fingertips run over the placket of his shirt. "There's so much we need to talk about." I grasped his wrist, wrapping his arm around me and placing my back toward him. "I'd like to find out, too."

He nodded, pulling my shoulders into his chest and resting his chin on top of my head. I could feel the rise and fall of his breaths as he looked out onto the ocean, and cleared his throat.

"The day Freddy died, the smoke coming from the grenade I threw was blue..."

Special Thanks

To the seven men from American Legion Post 927 and their PTSD support group, and Valor/Paul's House of Kunkletown, PA, who bravely opened up their lives, hearts, and stories to me so that I could accurately depict what it is like to experience PTSD as a war veteran.

Writing this novel wouldn't have been possible without you.

To my brother, Sgt. Daniel

For your indispensable knowledge and stories. I'm really proud of the person you've become, little brother, and appreciate you helping me bring this novel to life so much more than I could ever put into words.

Also, name your first baby after me or I take it back.

To all of those mentioned above, including the brave, selfless individuals who serve and protect our country each and every day.

Welcome home...

If you enjoyed reading THREE GRAY DOTS, *please* kindly leave a review letting me know! Then, find me on social media so I can share it with other fans! Reviews help so many other readers find good books, and I appreciate them so much!

Contact K.L. Randis

Kelly Randis, who goes by the pen name K.L. Randis, started journaling at age six and had short stories and poetry published by age thirteen. Randis found a lack of literature that described what a child had to go through when testifying against an abuser, particularly when the abuser was a parent. As an avid reader and journal-keeper, she penned the novel 'Spilled Milk*' to help future generations of children who were sexually abused navigate the court system.

She graduated from Penn State with a degree in Psychology and spent over four years in the mental health field. Spilled Milk is her first novel, which grabbed the #1 bestsellers spot on Amazon only twenty-four hours after its debut, where it has remained since 2015. Today, K.L. spends her days as a frequent commentator to news and media outlets, traveling to colleges & high schools for Q&As after they've read her novel, conducting military sexual assault trainings & speaking at the Pentagon, and working closely with professionals & legislators in social service and criminal justice fields—including non-profits— to bring about policy changes.

Randis remains a powerful keynote speaker for major events to inspire thousands in the community to donate, raising six figures in 2019 combined for the respective shelters, advocacy centers, and groups that hosted the events.

She remains very active on her social media channels, encouraging and advocating for those who may still be trying to find their own voice to speak out against childhood sexual abuse. Randis hosts a "Wellness Wednesday" via her Instagram stories every week for people to anonymously ask questions pertaining to a variety of subjects, including sexual abuse, child abuse, and mental health. Spilled Milk is required reading throughout the nation in both high school and college courses.

*Spilled Milk was based on true events. Author K.L. Randis testified at a criminal trial against her father, who was sentenced to prison for his crimes. He was sentenced to up to sixteen years in 2004.

Contact the Author:
Website: KLRandis.com
Email: authorklrandis@gmail.com
Facebook: facebook.com/klrandis
Spilled Milk Fan Page: facebook.com/spilledmilkrandis
Twitter: @KLRandis (https://twitter.com/klrandis)
Instagram: KLRandis (https://www.instagram.com/klrandis/?hl=en)
TikTok: @KLRandis (https://www.tiktok.com/@klrandis?lang=en)

Purchase signed copies for yourself
or a loved one at www.klrandis.com.

I love to stay in touch with my fans!

Subscribe to receive FREE samples (http://www.klrandis.com) of upcoming novels, delivered right to your email before they're released to the general public.
* Your information is never shared or sold.
Emails will be utilized for author news & giveaways only.

Other Books by K.L. Randis

View all books by visiting Amazon or www.klrandis.com.

Pillbillies (Pillbillies Series Book1)

When paramedics discover three-year-old Lacey floating in the bathtub and Jared Vorcelli barely conscious in his parents' living room, his drug addiction is put into the limelight and his pill-pushing days as a Kingpin of the Pocono Mountains come to a screeching halt. A chance meeting with a man named Dex opens a can of worms only Jared can close, as following a trail of red-speckled pills and green-tinted heroin become the only way to avenge his sister's death.

Laced (Pillbillies Series Book 2)

Exiled from his past life and plagued with the responsibility of a broken empire of Pillbillies, Jared Vorcelli dives into the underbelly of an addict's world to avenge the ones he loves and pull them from the wreckage of his choices. Targeting a dangerous ex-drug kingpin and his own father, Jared needs to learn who to trust, who to kill, and who to forgive when their respective paths collide.

Read on for a free sample of
bestselling novel by K.L. Randis, Spilled Milk

"I read this book in two days. I couldn't put it down."
— CHELSEA DEBOER, TEEN MOM 2

"This book has changed lives."
— GABRIELLE STONE, ACTRESS

"The honest, raw openness of your writing style is compelling.
Your story touched me deeply."
— JULIET PRITNER, ACTRESS, LAW & ORDER: SVU

"For the second year in a row, Kelly Randis will be using her first-
hand experience as a sexual assault survivor to educate national
leaders at the Pentagon, where she has been invited again as an
honorary guest for their sexual assault training."
— LT ASHLEY VALANZOLA, PENTAGON SEXUAL ASSAULT
PREVENTION

"Randis spoke to a full room of CASAs, attorneys, social workers,
and interested citizens about her personal story of sexual abuse at
the hands of her father and her inspirational triumph as a survivor."
— C.A.S.A (COURT APPOINTED SPECIAL ADVOCATES) OF
RICHMOND, VA

"You are an inspiration!"
— MARIO SCAVELLO, STATE SENATOR 40TH DISTRICT – PA

SPILLED MILK
Prologue

They never gave me a polygraph. I imagined myself strapped to a machine with a series of questions being rattled off. The proctors would nod their heads and mark the sheets as it fed out the results. Everyone wanted to know the truth, yet they asked the wrong questions over and over. "Are you okay?" "Do you need a break?" "What can I do?" No one would want to hear the real answers.

My hand closed around the organic chemistry note cards in my pocket. *How do hydrogen and chlorine react in the presence of an alkaline?*

The corner of my mouth twisted upward. Realizing it was inappropriate to laugh, I forced a serious face before anyone noticed. There I was, sitting in the District Attorney's office with stupid organic chemistry note cards in my pocket.

My mom sat against the adjacent wall from me staring off into space, a behavior I often mimicked myself. I never questioned the origin of my ability to transfix my eyes on an inanimate object while my brain sputtered into shutdown mode. It was a welcomed retreat at times.

Deep crevices muddled the brilliance of my mom's eyes and I wondered what she was thinking. Her weight shifted from one side of the chair then back again. It was a common dance she did to relieve the pressure in her lower back. The only interruption to her gaze happened when a man or woman wearing a suit entered the room.

I wondered if she even knew what organic chemistry was. "You would need this oxidizer. These two elements react like this, see?" I would draw a little diagram. "Simple."

"Oh, I don't know Brooke. You'll never need that anyway." The look on her face, the way her lips spread into a smaller, thin line told me she didn't want to hear about the things she refused to understand.

I was nineteen years old and a sophomore in college. The room could barely hold ten people and it was cement gray, just like I imagined when I thought of a courthouse waiting room. A secretary sat in the corner checking her email, only stopping to pick up the phone or take a long, hard swallow of her mega-sized WaWa coffee. She was the only one in the room that looked at ease, while everyone else sat in an awkward silence waiting for Heather to come in and tell us what was next.

I hate this room. My butt is asleep. Yes, Miss Secretary, can I help you? I'll just stare back.

Mismatched posters held to the wall with ripened shards of tape. My uncle's chair had one leg slightly shorter than the rest and his mindless rocking helped pass the time.

My aunt picked up a pamphlet sitting next to her and opened it. It returned to the table just as fast. STDs and their warning signs were not her choice of reading material.

Heather shuffled through the door with wide eyes, banging her briefcase against her knees. "Okay, good, everyone's here then."

She was my designated victim advocate. Her job was to guide me through the court hearings so I could understand, usually having to explain things to me more than once. The flood of information I was expected to absorb about the judicial system failed to hold any meaning to me.

Heather didn't try to sugarcoat anything. She was blunt. "This is what the judge means," followed by, "Any questions?"

Hundreds. Thousands even. I solved chemical reactions with ease but tripped over the things Heather tried to drill into my head. She was worn too.

"I don't know how you're doing this," Heather had said just a week earlier, her emerald eyes glazing over. "I give you a lot of credit kiddo.

They really tore you down in there and you kept your own. I know I keep saying this, but it'll be over soon."

I *would* get an Irish victim advocate. Her hair bounced around her face, blazing in a fireball of red glory while highlighting the doubt in her eyes as she tried to soothe me. I took it with a grain of salt, smiled, and accepted the one of many hugs that generally came my way after a debriefing.

She would often make some kind of remark about how us both being Irish was the only reason we would ever consider fighting so long and hard but that, "We make a great team, don't we?"

"You'd better come see me when all of this is over," she said. "You know, if you can ever handle coming back *here*," she motioned, flicking her hand into the space surrounding us.

She was right. I hated that room, the entire place: the smell of burnt coffee, the weird sounds the elevator made as we hurried down to courtroom three. I wanted to forget it all.

I had lost track of how many courtrooms I had testified in sometime after the first year of going there. Heather kept me grounded.

The security guards knew me well and were always happy to see me. The woman guard would greet me with a smile. "Ah, back again today?"

I would force a half-smile while scanning the lobby area. She would read my face. "He's not here yet, honey."

I relaxed and focused on getting into the District Attorney's office. The faster the better.

We parked behind the building and came through the less utilized handicapped entrance. Mom had rods and screws molded to her spine from a work injury years prior. She was a walking tin man, awkward gait included, guaranteed to set off the annoying alarm on the metal detectors. They waved a wand over her instead. She would nod and apologize for the inconvenience to the guards, but the smirk on her face absorbed all the pitied glances thrown her way.

Stroudsburg was a crumb-sized speck of a town in nowhere

Pennsylvania. Coming into the building through the back threw off any news reporters trying to overhear conversations between everyone that walked in with me.

"Well then," the guard would say, lowering her voice. "Let's hope I don't have to see you anymore after today." She would wink as I crossed the lobby to Heather's office.

"Doesn't my lawyer look like David Caruso? You know, the guy on CSI Miami? He's got reddish hair," I said to Heather, moving a hand over my own unruly mob of wavy hair. She checked him out and raised an approving eyebrow.

Even though he was my lawyer, I only exchanged a few words with him throughout our time together. Heather was the one to keep me updated on the important things and she would relay any information back to him that I needed him to know. Whenever I would enter his office his eyes would say, "I'm sorry you're here again".

I sometimes imagined him making those slam dunk speeches I saw on CSI. Secretly I wanted to witness the kind of closing statement that would leave the courtroom gasping, *I knew it! Case solved!* He remained quiet and collected though, boring even. I grimaced. I never wanted my life to end up like a TV show anyway. This was real life, *my life.*

The majority of my extended family showed up on the last day of court. I understood the drive from Long Island, New York to Pennsylvania was a long one. I didn't expect the support *every* time we had a hearing. That last day was important, though.

There was comfort in the waiting room, a sense of familiarity. Family stared at me and waited for me to cry, to think, to breathe.

Secretaries and lawyers, rushing in late to meet their first clients of the day, analyzed all of the people around me as they passed through. They only acknowledged the older adults, as if I were a commonplace child. I ignored them and studied my note cards, their eyes skimming over me as they wrongfully assessed my age and the reason I was there. They tightened their lips in pity.

Must be a custody hearing. Poor kid.

Chapter One

Wow, he can hold his breath for a long time.

My brother's head bobbed halfway under the surface of the kiddie pool. I traced the outline of Barbie's face on my bathing suit and waited for him to come up. Adam could hold his breath longer since he was seven, a whole year older than me. His mouth must have been bigger and could hold more air.

Oh well, I won the first two times we played who-can-hold-their-breath-the-longest. I guess he can win this one.

I poked his back between the shoulder blades to signal that I had come up for air and his head sank toward the bottom, rising again like a lazy balloon. He didn't budge.

"Come on Adam, you win. You can come up now."

The way his body drifted made the hairs on my neck feel funny. I stiffened a little.

Where's Dad? Does he see this?

Oh, there he is talking to the neighbor, probably about boring things. It's funny our neighbor's name is Cornelia. Good thing she's old, it sounds like an old name. I wouldn't even play with someone with a name like that, it sounds like the name of a vegetable or a disease. They're nice neighbors, I guess, but their dogs are mean. Maybe 'cause we tease them through the fence. I should tell Dad about Adam. If he yells at Adam to get up he definitely will. How is he holding his breath that long?

I climbed over the side of the pool and avoided dog poop as I crossed the lawn.

"Dad?"

I knew I shouldn't interrupt his adult conversation. This was important though; Adam couldn't stay underwater all day since we still had a fort to build. It was his turn to steal food from the pantry so we could hide and eat it. Sneaky older brother, I wasn't stupid. He always backed out of stealing food and then I would be forced to do it.

Not this time.

My dad kept talking to Cornelia about how Long Island wasn't what it used to be and how much he hated bills. "New York is an expensive place to live, I know, but how am I supposed to raise these kids and eventually send them to private school on one paycheck? Not to mention Molly didn't plan on breaking her back and disability only pays so much.

"Dad, I have to tell you something."

Cornelia looked down at me and smiled. *She's a pretty lady to have a disease for a name.*

Dad gave me the stare, the one that said "go away". I don't think I'd ever really seen his eyes because his glasses were so thick but I knew they were blue, like mine. My mom's were blue and all of us kids had blue eyes, so his had to be too. His were different though. His eyes never laughed.

"Yeah, what?"

Better make this fast. "I have to tell you something."

He blinked at me.

I pointed toward the pool. "Adam won't get up. And he already won the contest so..."

My dad was halfway across the yard before I even put my hand down. By the time I started running after him he already had Adam scooped up in his arms, face up on the ground beside the pool, and his beard pressed against his lips. They were the color of blueberries. Cornelia started screaming about an ambulance but I didn't see one. All I saw was Adam lying on the ground in his Ninja Turtles bathing suit.

What a faker. He doesn't have to fake to get attention, I already know he won.

Adam started coughing and water came out of his mouth at the same time he started crying. "Daddy!" he gasped. His white knuckles grabbed at Dad's shirt. I started crying too because it seemed like the right thing to do and I didn't realize that Adam was really in trouble until just then.

My dad helped Adam to his feet. "That's all I need, another bill for an ambulance. It's not like I have insurance or anything. Brooke, get next door and tell Cornelia she better not call an ambulance. He's fine."

Cornelia didn't look happy but I did as I was told and ran back home. Adam was still sucking in deep swallows of air as tears slid down his cheek and a Popsicle stood hostage in his left hand. My dad sat at the kitchen table, his hands shaking as he sipped his water.

Look at him, my dad. He just saved Adam's life. I bet he would save mine too if I needed it. I bet he would do anything for us.

My feet stuck to the grimy kitchen floor as I crossed the room and grabbed my dad's arms to open them so I could crawl into his lap. I wrapped my arms around his neck and put my cheek against his scruffy face. He always smelled like machines. Mom said it was because he worked hard all day, putting them together and fixing the broken ones.

"Let's not tell Mom about this, snuggle bug." He pulled me into his chest with one arm and took another sip of his water.

Adam's near drowning would be the first of many secrets I would keep for my dad. "I won't, Daddy."

I put my head on his chest. I knew why he didn't want me to tell. Mom would be upset that she missed Dad saving Adam's life. She would have wanted to see it happen too, like I did, so she could remember all her of life how great he is, like I will.

Chapter Two

I was seven.

All I knew about a CB radio was that Mom and Dad met on one and after a week of talking they decided to meet up at Jones Beach. It took them over an hour to find each other since New York's beaches that stretched the length of Long Island were often packed on the blazing summer weekends.

My aunt had already landed her beau-to-be and had a wedding planned for that October. Not wanting to be outdone, Mom moved in with David after a few short weeks of dating. They wed in September and planned the house, the two kids, and the white picket fence. Three kids, two bug infested apartments and a cramped unkempt ranch on a desolate dead-end street later, I finished a glass of milk and readied my next question.

"So, what's a CB?" I asked.

After I watched a cartoon about two giraffes in love, I realized I didn't even know how my parents met. The giraffes flirted through a lyrical orchestra of words and sing-alongs. I imagined that's what my mom felt like when she fell in love.

Mom looked up from the tea bag she had fished out of her mug, trying not to burn her fingers. "Uh, it's a way people used to meet each other. You would talk over the radio and get to know people you wouldn't normally meet. It was a new kind of technology then. Everyone was doing it," she assured me. "I wasn't the only one."

I remained motionless. *Keep going.*

She took a sip of her tea. I stared at her.

"Why? You doing a book report or something?"

"No."

I watched the ash dangling from her cigarette threaten to drop onto the table before turning away. It was always the same. Unless there was a reason, questions were to be kept to a minimum. She went back to her tea, ending the conversation. I left to find Adam.

He was cross-legged on the floor playing with his K'Nex set when I walked into the living room. I leaned against the neglected grand piano and cleared my throat. "You'll never guess how Mom and Dad met." My arms folded across my chest and I shifted my weight. "Mom just told me."

"Through a CB," he said, without looking up.

"Not-uh." *Why does he always know everything?*

He stared at me.

"How do *you* know?" I said.

We were fifteen months apart in age which meant everything was a competition; who could read all the Disney books the fastest, ride their bike further or know all answers to the universe both large and small. I studied Adam as he focused on jamming a long yellow connector into a blue corner piece.

Ha, that's not gonna fit. He needs the green connector. Stupid.

He would sit there for hours in his solitude and craft the most magnificent things: ferris wheels, cars, and the Empire State Building. Sometimes I would play with him, but building houses and cars that were destroyed by Dad's work boots got boring.

"I found an old box in the garage a few months ago. It looked like a radio so I took it apart because it looked broken," he said. He shifted onto his knees to search for another piece.

"So how'd you know that's how Mom and Dad met then?" My eyes glanced over the holes in his sneakers. His t-shirt swam around arms no thicker than sticks.

Adam had a way of making me feel like I should always know his exact thoughts, and that it was some great inconvenience for him to have to explain anything. I shifted from one foot to another, raised my eyebrows, and sighed loud enough to wake a sleeping baby. He fished around for a random piece, skipping over the green one I knew he needed.

Over the years I learned that as long as I was quiet and let him think I was seriously concerned about not having a clue to what he was talking about, he'd save me and let me in on the thoughts running through his head.

After a minute Adam pushed one of his sleeves up above his shoulder blade. There was a white scar the size of a grain of rice on the back of his shoulder. He rubbed it thoughtfully before his eyes met mine. "I showed Dad how cool the inside of the box was, there were all these wires and stuff. He told me I broke the CB him and Mom met on. She was keeping it, I guess. He pushed me into the wall. Mom's garden scissors cut me."

"Oh."

Mom tripped over a toy fire truck as she entered the room. "Hey—*Adam*," she said, looking at all the scattered pieces on the floor. You could barely see the spinach colored carpet beneath the toys, random pieces of clothing, and clutter everywhere. The cramped room could barely hold the piano, sofa, and TV. "I thought I told you to put this away? Now let's go. Put this away, *now*." She picked up a toy, decided she didn't know where she could relocate it to, and put it back down again. "We're not going anywhere unless this room is spotless. You have five minutes."

Adam practiced his lawyer skills. "Mom, I *only* have to finish this one piece."

"Where we goin' Mom?" I asked.

"Grandma's. Grandpa's making dinner so once Thomas wakes up from his nap and after Kat eats—Adam I said *now*." She shoved a pile of plastic pieces into a heap with her foot.

"But Moooom," Adam said. "It's not fair. All I need to do is this *one piece.*"

The thought of going to Grandma's was exhilarating. My knees hit the floor beside Adam and I searched for the part he needed. His eyes widened. "Hey! Hey Mom she's messing up my stuff!"

"I'm helping."

"No you're *not*. You don't even know what I'm looking for!"

Mom is going to yell in two seconds. Where IS it?

I locked eyes with the green connector and reached for it. The structure now complete, I looked toward Adam. His head dropped and he turned on his heel. "I knew I needed that piece. I didn't need your help to find it."

"Can we go now?" I asked.

Mom hustled Adam, Thomas, Kat and me into the minivan. We spent ten minutes driving down Southern State Highway before we pulled up in front of my grandparents' impressive, white Victorian home. Engraved columns hovered around the garden on the side of the house and the lawn was zebra striped from a fresh cut; it meant Grandpa was expecting us. He was nowhere to be seen, but if I had to guess he was probably in the backyard skimming the swimming pool. Oak trees that lined the property kept him busy during the fall and summer months between his weekly pool and grass preservations.

My seat belt was unbuckled and I jumped over the seat in front of me before Mom put the van in park. The metal door handle fumbled in my hands before I rushed it open and jumped off the platform of the van onto the grass.

Grandma came to the front door before I could call out to see if Grandpa was still lingering in the garden. "Grandma!" I said, and ran full speed to the front porch.

"Hey, sugar!" she said as I tackled her waist. She wrapped me in a soft hug and pulled me closer. Her perfume danced around my face and she tightened her grip.

"How's my girl?" she asked. Grandma's hugs were always so genuine, so warm.

Before I could answer, Mom was walking up the porch steps and handing Kat over. "Careful, she's doing the projectile spit up thing again," she warned. Grandma held outstretched arms and took the baby while Adam zigzagged around her. Thomas waddled behind him, stopping to put a dandelion in his mouth.

"Hi Grandma!" Adam called out. He dashed into the house and I heard the wooden toy chest creak open in the front room. My grandpa had built him a custom toy box when he was just two years old, but my mom said the stain he had used on the cedar wood gave Adam an allergic reaction. Grandpa had spent weeks building it, even detailing the top in bright white letters that spelled out his name. Now it was tucked under the window of their front room, waiting for us whenever we came over.

My grandma moved us into the living room. "I just had the carpet shampooed, sorry if it's still damp. Just put the diaper bag on one of the flowered couches, Molly."

Symmetrical paintings depicting the ocean floated above each couch. I wandered over to the wood stove and looked up at the mantle filled with pictures of family, grandkids, and knickknacks from the beach.

I sunk into a couch and stared up at the ceiling that seemed to go on forever. The room smelled and felt like Grandma. "My goodness, look at how big everyone is getting," Grandma said. She put Kat on the living room floor. "I *think* that somebody's birthday is coming up, but I can't remember who." She met my eyes with a smile.

"Me! It's my birthday Grandma. I'm turning eight." I smiled.

She remembered.

"Oh it *is?*" she exclaimed, bringing her hand to her forehead. "Well I guess we'll just need to go to Toys R Us while everyone else swims then."

"Oh Mom, no," Mom started, shaking her head, "not necessary." She handed Kat a stuffed bear and pulled a pill bottle out of her pocket. Two oval shaped, cream colored pills fell into her hand. With a fluid motion she popped them into her mouth and threw her head back.

Now you see them, now you don't.

I had heard my mom repeat the story of how she hurt her back thousands of times. She had worked as a nurse's aide at Great Side Hospital in lower Manhattan. Her shifts were sporadic, and having four small children at home made it difficult to juggle everything.

She managed to generate a significant income working around Dad's work schedule. They had asked her to work a double shift a few weeks before Christmas and she obliged, making a quick last-minute call to the babysitter.

A heavy-set man had just come out of surgery for gallstones and she assisted in transporting him to his room. The registered nurse left the room suddenly, telling my mom not to move him until she came back with more help. She hurried out before my mom could protest otherwise.

The man groggily tried to shift himself from the cot to the bed on his own. His weight fought against him, and he began to slip in between the two beds. Mom acted on instinct and pushed against the cot to catch him between the two beds instead of letting him fall to the floor.

Two nurses walked into the room a second too late and scrambled over to help just as Mom fell to the floor from the pressure. She herniated and ruptured seven discs in her back; doctors were sure she would never be pain or painkiller free for the rest of her life.

She had saved her job by doing the right thing and she saved the hospital from a major lawsuit. In return, she became a permanently disabled mother to four children, eventually succumbing to such intense chronic pain after five back surgeries that she started collecting social security disability and had to leave her job permanently.

I remember one day I watched a girl run off of the school bus and her mom swooped her up and swung her around in a tight hug, backpack attached and all. The mom kissed her head as she set her down, eyes bright and chatting about how her day was. My eyes welled up. I came home and accused my mom of not loving me.

"Why can't you pick *me* up?" I cried. "I'm the smallest one in my class, I'm little!"

Mom started crying too. "Oh, Brooke, I'm sorry. I just...can't." She gripped the edges of her back brace with white knuckles.

I couldn't even sit in her lap as I sobbed. My only comfort was to stand next to her while she sat at the kitchen table and bury my face in her shirt until I had nothing left to cry.

That day I learned to let go of things like being picked up and feeling hugs that squished my bones. Instead, I focused on giving those things to Adam, Thomas, and Kat. I wanted to feel that closeness, even if I was the one who had to initiate it.

"Oh no, no, I want to. I insist she pick something for her birthday," Grandma beamed, watching my mom swallow her pills. She turned to me. "You ready, sugar? Let's go."

We talked about the beach and my upcoming birthday as she merged onto the highway. "So, tell me everything, what grade are you going into?" she asked.

The only time I stopped talking the entire ride was to ask her what she thought about the rule of checking out *only* three books from the library at a time. I was pleased to find we shared the same opinion of it being totally unfair.

As we pulled into the parking lot of Toys R Us she asked me what I wanted. "I'm not sure," I said. I tapped my foot and waited for Grandma to turn off the car. The store was full of beautiful dolls, board games, and costumes. I was headed right for the notorious pink aisle all of the girls at school talked about.

Grandma held my hand as we crossed the parking lot and gave it a little squeeze as the double door opened in front of us. "Whatever you want," she said. She meant it.

I sped past the clearance toys and stuffed animals. The Barbie aisle was a short distance from the outdoor play section. Grandma strolled close behind me. "Oh, look at *this* one," I said. Princess Barbie was off of the shelf and cradled against my chest. Swim Team Barbie stared at me. "Or *this* one. Grandma she has a bathing suit, she can swim with me."

Grandma laughed. "She can! Whatever one you want, take your time."

Each doll's face and features had to be considered along with the extras each doll came with: a stroller, an umbrella, and binoculars. There were so many. I lined up three choices next to each other and studied them. School Teacher Barbie won; she came with a blackboard and real chalk. "This one," I said, and handed it to Grandma.

"Excellent choice."

She took my hand and headed toward the registers. I let her cruise me around passing people and aisles so I could study my Barbie's clothes inside the box. A toddler down one aisle threw himself on the ground in protest over a matchbox car. The checkout lane was a few feet in front of us when I saw something. I tugged on Grandma's hand. "Wait. Grandma, can I look at something?"

She checked her watch. "Sure sugar, quick though. Grandpa should have started the grill by now."

An end aisle with a clearance display caught my attention. I picked up a small book with Disney's Aladdin and Jasmine on the cover, turning it over in my hand. A jingle from the side forced a smile. A small, silver lock clasped the front and back of the book together. My eyes widened. "Grandma, I want *this* instead."

I handed it over and Grandma flipped it from front to back. She checked the price, a mere $3.99, and gave me a crooked smile. "This?" she asked. "Do you know what it's for?"

"It's a journal," I said. I saw them on TV and read about them, but I never had one. It was a real journal, with a lock to keep all thoughts and secrets forever bound to the person who wrote in it. "Please, Grandma?" I asked. I tried to read her face.

She looked at the Barbie in one hand and journal in the other. She thought for a minute, and then bent down until her blue eyes were level with mine. "If you *really* want it and *only* if you promise to write in it every day, until it's completely full," she bargained.

My heart skipped. "Every single day," I promised.

"Okie dokie." She stood up and tucked the Barbie on a nearby shelf, shaking her head. "Of all the things in this store, it doesn't surprise me." She put the journal on the conveyor belt and paid with a crisp five-dollar bill.

We got back to the house just as Grandpa was pulling burgers and hot dogs off of the grill. I rushed inside, eager to show Mom and Adam my present. "Look what Grandma got me!" I gave it to Mom and wiggled in next to Adam on the patio bench to eat a cheeseburger.

"Oh?" Mom said. She flipped it over. "Mom, you took her to Toys R Us and got her a book?"

"It's what she wanted," Grandma said. She shrugged, taking a seat next to Kat and Grandpa. "She's the birthday girl."

"It's not a book *Mom*, it's a *journal*," I corrected. Lemonade dribbled down my chin. "Grandpa, Grandma got me a journal and I have to write in it every day. I will too, I'll write on every page."

"Mmm," he said in agreement, putting ketchup on his burger. "Good."

Grandpa wouldn't have been a very good journal keeper. He didn't talk much. It's usually what he didn't say that said a lot.

After dinner Adam and I swam in the pool while the adults poured drinks into glasses shaped like tennis balls. Grandpa's brow was pressed together as he stood next to Mom's chair. He was telling her something important, I knew, because he shook his finger at her as he talked. Grandma brought us ice pops a short time later and we sat next to the adults to eat them.

Grandpa still had a perplexed look on his face and tried to give Mom some money. "You need it, just take it Molly," he demanded.

Grandpa didn't like it when Mom turned down his ideas. She gave a brief rebuttal before he stuffed the bills into her purse. He mumbled for a few more minutes and finally excused himself from the table to check his tomato plants.

When it was time to leave I thanked Grandma again for the journal and tucked it under my arm. "Remember your promise," she said, winking at me and giving me a final hug. I couldn't wait to get home to write in it.

We pulled up in front of our unimpressive ranch. Dad's car was absent from the driveway. "I'm putting Kat to bed," Mom called over her shoulder. "Adam, help Thomas inside and clean up these toys before your father gets home. Brooke, load the dishwasher would you?" Kat slumped over Mom's shoulder like a hefty rag doll, puffing out breaths of air.

I lugged a kitchen chair over to the sink. Once I was level with the countertop, I picked dried spaghetti off of plates and splashed water inside the cups that had sour milk. The liquid soap container weighed down my arm but I finally managed to pour some into the square tray of the dishwasher. The sink was empty ten minutes later, and I used my shirt as a towel.

The front door opened and I heard heavy boots in the hallway. Dad was home.

TO CONTINUE READING,
visit klrandis.com for more information.

"I read this book in two days. I couldn't put it down."
— CHELSEA DEBOER, TEEN MOM 2

"This book has changed lives."
— GABRIELLE STONE, ACTRESS

"The honest, raw openness of your writing style is compelling. Your story touched me deeply."
— JULIET PRITNER, ACTRESS, LAW & ORDER: SVU

"For the second year in a row, Kelly Randis will be using her first-hand experience as a sexual assault survivor to educate national leaders at the Pentagon, where she has been invited again as an honorary guest for their sexual assault training."
— LT ASHLEY VALANZOLA, PENTAGON SEXUAL ASSAULT PREVENTION

"Randis spoke to a full room of CASAs, attorneys, social workers, and interested citizens about her personal story of sexual abuse at the hands of her father and her inspirational triumph as a survivor."
— C.A.S.A (COURT APPOINTED SPECIAL ADVOCATES) OF RICHMOND, VA

"You are an inspiration!"
— MARIO SCAVELLO, STATE SENATOR 40TH DISTRICT – PA

Made in the USA
Middletown, DE
02 June 2022